THE TOURIST IS TOAST

A HUMOROUS PARANORMAL COZY MYSTERY

CARLY WINTER

Edited by
DIVAS AT WORK EDITING
Cover by
COVEREDBYMELINDA.COM

WESTWARD PUBLISHING / CARLY FALL, LLC

A tourist is shoved from a cliff. It's up to an unruly ghost to solve the murder.

When Bernie and her ghostly grandmother, Ruby, witness the killing of a tourist from a far, they find themselves ensnared in a vengeful group of suspects, each having an excellent motive for pushing the man to his death.

Deputy Adam Gallagher has been assigned to solve the case. The problem? No one is talking. When Ruby approaches Bernie with a secret plan to nail the murderer and help Adam, Bernie reluctantly agrees.

As Bernie and Ruby do their part to assist Adam, Bernie realizes the case is far more complicated than anyone thought. Unraveling it may put them all in danger. Can she find the murderer and get the dead man justice before the killer gets to her first?

CHAPTER ONE

What should one wear to meet a ghost for the first time?

The question spun in my mind as I stared at the eighties T-shirts hanging in my closet. Was I in a *Back to the Future* mood? Or *The Breakfast Club*?

"Hurry up, Bernie," my dead grandmother's ghost said from the kitchen. "We're going to be late!"

With a sigh, I grabbed *The Breakfast Club* and pulled it over my head, then hurried into the bathroom to run a brush through my hair.

"Bernie!"

"I'm coming, Ruby! Quit hassling me! You're stressing me out!"

She muttered something about everything in my

life causing me anxiety, and she wasn't wrong. I tended to be a worrier.

When I found my reflection presentable, I walked out to the kitchen, where Ruby waited for me. About my height, her slim ghostly form was covered in a purple mumu, her long gray hair parted down the middle and held at the nape in a ponytail.

"Let's go!" she said, turning on her heel and racing toward the front door. "I have a good vibe about today!"

I wish I shared her enthusiasm. Frankly, I could barely handle dealing with one ghost, and the thought of being able to see and communicate with two seemed so far out of my realm of comfort, it made me uneasy.

This was our fourth time going to Deputy Adam Gallagher's condominium to attempt to find his ghost. Well, he didn't know if he truly had one, but he did have a strong hunch, as well as a belief that Ruby and I would be able to coax the entity out of hiding. We hadn't exactly been successful.

"I feel like we need outfits for our ghost hunting," Ruby said. "Like they had in *Ghostbusters*. Except overalls aren't very flattering. Maybe something that shows a little leg and cleavage, though."

And she wouldn't be able to wear said outfit.

She'd died in her purple mumu and that was apparently how she'd spend eternity.

"Are we walking again?" Ruby asked, her voice tinted with a slight whine.

"Yes," I replied as I locked the front door to my bed and breakfast. "I need the exercise."

"That's what you always say."

"That's because it's true," I muttered. My jeans had begun to feel a little tight. I blamed my new love of sugary treats from Sarah's Smoothies.

"You aren't fat, honey," Ruby said.

"Not yet, anyway," I mumbled. "That's what I'm trying to prevent. Let's go."

While I was apprehensive of meeting the ghost supposedly residing at Adam's house, Ruby seemed to be quite excited by the prospect. I wasn't sure if it was because going to Adam's meant she got to leave my bed and breakfast, or if she really wanted to meet another entity like her.

Unfortunately, she couldn't move beyond the walls of my home without me. Neither of us could explain it, but there was some sort of tether that bound us together—while inside the house, she wandered freely, including to a place she called her tunnel. I had no way to access it, but from her description, it sounded like some sort of gateway to heaven. She'd come to the conclusion they wouldn't let her in, which didn't surprise me. Ruby had lived a pretty rambunctious life, and she may not be considered heavenly material.

As I walked down the street, Ruby floated next to me humming a Rolling Stones tune. She skipped and twirled around, not having a care in the world. Understandable, considering she was dead. She'd had very few concerns while alive, and the afterlife had brought the number down to a hard zero.

"Summer's coming!" she sang as we arrived at Adam's complex. "Time to slip into the old bikini and check out the college hotties at Slide Rock!"

That's what *she* would have done while alive. Being in my mid-thirties, 'college hotties' were not on my radar. Ogling young men seemed wrong on many levels and definitely had a high *eww* factor. I had nothing in common with an eighteen-year-old, and I certainly didn't want to spend my days pounding down beers.

Besides, I now tried to avoid the summer sun as much as I could. Temperatures would soar into the high nineties in Sedona, Arizona, which was nothing compared to the earth-scorching heat down in the valley. The Phoenix area was well-known for their three-digit temperatures during the summer months.

However, I tended to burn fairly easily, so I tried to hide from the sun as much as possible. Skin cancer, wrinkles... I did my best to escape fun things like that.

"I'll be staying indoors, thank you," I said. "I don't need to get another burn in my lifetime."

"That's what suntan lotion is for!" Ruby replied.

"I don't want skin cancer."

"Oh, jeez, Bernie," Ruby muttered while we approached Adam's door. "What in the world am I going to do with you?"

Ignoring her, I ran a hand over my hair and quickly wiped away the beads of sweat that had gathered on my brow before knocking.

"Fine. Pay me no attention," she said, then ghosted right through the door. She wouldn't go far because of our tether, but I heard her yelling.

"Come on out, you big, wimpy jerk!"

If Adam did have a spirit in his house, Ruby was apparently done trying to kindly coax it out as she had before and had resorted to name calling.

I sighed as Adam opened the door. "Hey," he said, glancing all around me while running a hand through his blond hair. "Is she here?"

He meant Ruby, of course. "Yes. She's behind

you, yelling for your ghost to show herself. Or himself."

Adam glanced over his shoulder then waved me in. "I didn't smell her."

No one but me could hear or see Ruby, but an encounter was usually accompanied by the scent of lavender and marijuana, which happened to be exactly what Ruby had smelled like while alive.

"You're an even worse ghost than me!" Ruby continued as she spun around in a circle with her hands on her hips. "At least I don't hide in a corner like a frightened little puppy!"

"What's she saying?" Adam asked as his gaze flittered around the room.

"She's basically calling him or her a wimp."

Adam furrowed her brow. "That's not exactly friendly. I hope it doesn't make the ghost upset."

"Loser! Come out, loser!"

"It will probably be quite upset," I said, crossing my arms over my chest as Ruby continued to yell at the ghost. If there truly was one.

I'd had a secret crush on Adam for months and we were finally getting to know each other. Never once did I consider that he would want me and Ruby to help him flush out a ghost from his condo, but there I stood. When he first approached me with the idea of us helping him, he'd claimed things were moved around. I'd yet to witness that happening, but I also didn't know if I would be able to actually see the ghost. After all, I hadn't been able to see Ruby until I'd been hit by lightning and knocked out cold.

As Ruby continued to scream insults, Adam and I looked around the tidy living room for some sign of her abuse being effective. I appreciated his panache for cleanliness as my OCD kicked in at the sight of messes. Even the pillows had been lined up nicely on the brown leather couch and the books sat in the bookcase according to height. I'd never mentioned anything, yet I couldn't help but wonder if he had a bit of OCD himself.

"Do you see anything?" he whispered.

I shook my head.

"Come over here, Bernie," Ruby said. "Maybe the wuss is hiding in the bedrooms."

Since Ruby couldn't go more than fifteen feet away from me when not in our house, I followed her down the hall so she could hurl insults at the bedroom walls.

"Has she found him?" Adam asked, trailing behind me.

"No. She's looking, though. She thinks he's in the back."

We'd been through this before the last three times we visited. After the second time, I had my doubts about the ghost. After the third, I considered the whole exercise a waste of time. Yet, it gave me an excuse to be with Adam, so I'd keep coming as long as he wanted us there.

Ruby entered his bedroom and began to search under the forest-green bedspread and in the closet while Adam and I stood in the doorway. I sighed when she began to shout into the closet.

"Is she at it again?" Adam asked.

"Yes. If I were your ghost, I wouldn't show myself either."

Adam chuckled, his blue eyes seeming to sparkle as he stared at me. "Listen, I have tomorrow off, and I was wondering if you'd be interested in going on a hike or an ATV ride."

My heart thundered as Ruby came out of the closet. Time alone with Adam? Sign me up!

"You can't go, Bernie," Ruby said. "Remember you're worried about sunburns?"

I ignored her and smiled. "I'd love to. I'm game for either, so you choose which you'd prefer."

Ruby snorted and crossed her arms over her chest. "So I guess you're willing to get sunburn for him, but not for me? You'd choose a cop over me? Over hunky college boys?"

"Maybe an ATV ride?" Adam said, brushing his hand over my bare arm and sending goosebumps over my skin.

"If you go on an ATV ride, you need to take me!" Ruby said. "You know I love the ATV!"

Of course I was aware of that. I remembered tearing through town on her ATV she'd named Flash when I'd come and spend the summers with her as a kid and young teen.

"An ATV ride sounds great," I said.

"Bernie, take me!" Ruby said, dropping to her knees and holding her hands in a prayer position, her ghost-hunting forgotten. "Please, please, pretty please!"

I glanced down at her and then back at Adam, torn. My gut said to leave her at home, but my heart told me to invite her. She'd spent three years after her death on this plane without being seen, without being able to leave our house. Neither of us understood why she was trapped, and I felt bad for her.

And honestly, I didn't think I could take the guilt trip she'd lay on me.

"Would you mind if Ruby came along?" I asked, my cheeks flaming with embarrassment. It wasn't every day I asked if I could bring my dead grand-mother's ghost on a date.

Adam laughed again and nodded. "That's fine. I remember you telling me she likes ATVs."

Ruby jumped to her feet. "Woohoo!" I tried to ignore her dancing. "Thanks, honey!" she said. "Even though rule number five of life is to never date a cop, this one may not be too bad."

I pursed my lips together to hide my smile.

"What did she say?" Adam asked, narrowing his gaze as he stared into the bedroom. "I wish I could see and hear her."

Ruby walked over and stood about a foot away from Adam. "Yeah, he may be a keeper. You have to watch him. In my experience, cops are bad news boyfriends."

While alive, Ruby had dated Adam's boss, Sheriff Bruce Walker. Considering her enjoyment of illegal activities, the relationship hadn't been smooth and joyous.

"It doesn't look like your ghost is going to make an appearance," I said. "Do you want to go grab a cup of coffee?"

"I'd like that, but I do need to get to work," Adam replied, taking my hand in his. "Rain check?"

"Sure thing."

"Let's get out of here," Ruby said. "I think old lover boy here is making this stuff up so he can get you in the sack. I don't think this ghost is real."

Rolling my eyes, I turned to head down the hallway when a blast of cold air hit my back. As I glanced into the bedroom, a book rose from the bookcase and flew across the room, missing Ruby by inches. It hit me square in the forehead.

Stunned for a brief second, I gasped and glanced at the bookcase, then my knees gave out. Just as I sank to the carpet, I heard a man's voice... one that didn't belong to Adam. "Of course I'm real, you obnoxious banshee."

As Adam helped me to my feet, I studied his bedroom, looking for the offending spirit.

"Sorry about that," the voice said. "I hit the wrong one. My apologies, miss."

"Did you hear that?" I whispered.

"Was he saying he meant for the book to hit me?" Ruby asked.

I nodded as Adam said, "I didn't hear a thing, but the book... jeez, Bernie. Are you okay?" He led me over to the bed and I sat down, my breath coming in short spurts as my gaze darted around the room while he touched my forehead. "You aren't bleeding, but it looks like you're going to have a bruise."

"You definitely have a ghost," I said. "And yes, Ruby, that book was meant for you."

"I'm sorry you got hit, Bernie," she said with a chuckle. "But at least we know this place is haunted."

"Let me get you some ice," Adam said, rushing from the room.

"Who are you?" Ruby yelled. "Show yourself, you coward! Throwing books at young women... what the heck is wrong with you? Come out here so I can shove this book right up your—"

"It's okay, Ruby," I said. "Please don't agitate him any further."

"Are you sure? Because I'd love nothing more than to feed him my knuckle sandwich." She made two fists and held them up, boxer style.

"Yes. Please, just sit down."

I patted the bed next to me and she hurried over.

"Are you sure you're okay, Bernie?"

"I'll be fine."

Adam rushed in as a headache began to form.

"Lie down," he instructed. "We can place the icepack right across your forehead."

I shut my eyes when my head hit the mattress. The coolness of the icepack calmed my throbbing head and nerves.

After a few minutes, I decided I'd go to sleep if I didn't get moving. "Thanks for this," I said, sitting up and handing Adam the icepack.

"I'm sorry this happened to you," he said. "The ghost has never done anything... violent before."

"It wasn't your fault," I replied, my gaze sliding pointedly over to Ruby. "I think he was badgered just a little too much."

"He?"

"Yes," I replied. "It's a male."

"I wouldn't have had to do that if he'd shown himself the first three times we came over here," Ruby said with a huff. "I'm all about getting results. The definition of stupidity is doing the same thing over and over and expecting a different turnout. I had to up my ghost-busting game a little. It was a tactical change."

"Are you sure you're okay?" Adam asked.

My head spun a little as I rose from the bed. "I'll be fine."

"Do you still want to go tomorrow? If not, I understand."

No, there would be no canceling our date. "Of course I want to go. I'm excited."

He continued to apologize while we walked to the front door.

"Adam, please. It's okay. I'm going to be fine. At least we know you aren't losing your mind and you do indeed have a ghost."

He nodded and shook his head. "Yeah, I'm relieved about that. But I wonder who it is and why he's in my condo?"

CHAPTER TWO

The next day Ruby and I had plans to meet Adam at Jumping Jack's Jeep Tours for a late afternoon / early evening ride. Adam had an ATV of his own, but I'd been forced to sell Ruby's when I first moved to Sedona. I was saving up for another, but I didn't quite have enough to purchase. So, I'd rent.

To Ruby's chagrin, we walked and arrived a few minutes early. Jack greeted me in the lot while wiping his hands with a black-grease-stained rag. With his wavy brown hair, green eyes, and bright smile, he was definitely one of the most popular men in town. "Hey, Bernie!"

"Well hello, Mr. Dimples," Ruby purred. "Aren't you looking sexy today?"

And yes, he had dimples.

I pursed my lips and tried to ignore her. "Hi, Jack. I was hoping to rent an ATV today."

"What happened to your head?" he asked, the smell of oil surrounding him. Not only did he rent ATVs, but also hosted the Jeep tours and fixed all the vehicles.

As predicted, I'd ended up with a bruise right in the middle of my forehead, accompanied by a lump. "I ran into an open cupboard."

"You better watch out where you're going from now on," he said with a chuckle.

"Very true."

"I have an ATV available. C'mon inside and I'll get the paperwork ready."

Ruby and I followed him into the office. "If only I was alive," she said with a sigh.

"If only you were forty years younger," I muttered.

"Age is nothing but a number," Ruby retorted. "I could show this handsome man a thing or two."

"Please don't," I murmured, holding up my palm. "Don't go there."

Jack glanced over his shoulder. "Did you say something?"

"No," I replied. It was always so hard with Ruby around. First, she had no boundaries. Second, she didn't possess a filter and always said exactly was on her mind, which was often inappropriate. Third, I wanted to answer and often found myself speaking to her when I shouldn't. It would only be a matter of time before people in this town began to gossip about the bed and breakfast owner who strolled down the street muttering to herself, if they didn't already.

As I filled out the paperwork, I heard an engine rumbling out front. I glanced over my shoulder to find Adam arriving on his ATV wearing a backpack. I should have brought my own filled with water, but I'd been in such a hurry, it had slipped my mind. Jack went out to greet him—they'd been friends for quite a while.

"All done," I said, laying the clipboard and my credit card on Jack's desk. I walked over and picked a helmet, trying not to think who had worn it before me. Even though Jack cleaned them after each use, I needed to buy my own before I bought an ATV because wearing a public one gave me the heebie-jeebies. "Let's head out." Besides OCD tendencies, I could probably be classified as a germaphobe.

Ruby hummed as she trailed me, and I joined the men.

"Depending on where you two go, I may see you out there," Jack said. "I've got a full moon tour."

"I didn't know it was the full moon," Adam said. "That'll be pretty."

"Yeah, when it comes up and you're by the cliffs, it's almost magical," Jack replied, shaking his head. "Makes you really think about God and stuff."

I'd never seen Jack being philosophical or religious, so this new side of him surprised me. Perhaps there was more to him than dimples and nice eyes.

"I'll let you two get moving."

"My credit card is on your desk," I said. "I'll grab it when we come back."

"Perfect." Jack pulled a set of keys out of his pocket. "I'll keep it in my safe. You can take the ATV with the blue tag right over there. It's gassed up and ready to go. Even put in a new starter this morning."

"Wait a minute," Adam said. "I'm paying for this."

"It's fine, Adam," I said. "You have an ATV and I don't. I'm happy to pay for my own."

I grabbed the keys from Jack just as Ruby said, "Look over there. Dumb Darla Darling giving you the evil eye."

Glancing over at the diner, I saw her staring out the window of her establishment at us. My ex-friend seemed certain I was trying to take away her boyfriend, Jack. I had no intention of doing so, but she still stared daggers at me. The whole thing was quite childish. What were we? Fifteen, not thirty-five?

When Jack headed inside and was out of earshot, I turned to Adam. "Did you see your ghost again?"

He shook his head. "I kept waiting for something to happen, but nothing ever did. It was creepy. How's your bruise?"

"It's fine. Better than it looks."

"I'm really sorry about that."

I laughed and gently touched my forehead. "Please quit apologizing. It's not like you can control your ghost. I can't control mine."

"No one controls me," Ruby said. "No matter if I'm alive or dead. Now, can we please kill the chatter and get moving?"

"Are you ready to head out?" Adam asked, unaware of Darla's hateful stare across the parking lot.

Pretending I didn't see her, I slipped on my sunglasses and helmet. "Yes, let's go."

"Woohoo!" Ruby yelled as I straddled the ATV and she got comfortable behind me. A shiver went down my spine at her presence. "Let's blow this popsicle stand!"

I followed the speed limit with Adam trailing me

through town, keeping with the flow of traffic. Ruby, who loved speed, grumbled about me abiding by the laws, but I ignored her. When we came to the trailhead, I pulled over and waited for Adam who had gotten caught at the last light.

Ruby sighed impatiently. "Last time we went for a ride you thought Jack was trying to kill you. Remember?"

I nodded. "This time there isn't a murder, so hopefully it'll be much more fun for us."

"Unless the copper wants to throw cold water on a good day and keep us at a snail's pace. I told you to never date cops. They're snoozers."

"Ruby, Adam is a great guy. The problem with you dating Sheriff Walker was that his job is to uphold the laws you were determined to break. I, on the other hand, appreciate and respect laws. They're there for a reason."

"To break them!" Ruby bellowed and began to cackle.

Adam pulled up a moment later. "Sorry about that. I got cut off in traffic."

"No worries." I smiled. I'd wait all day for him if needed.

"You're so smitten with this guy," Ruby said. "Just gag me with a fork, will you?"

"A spoon."

"What?"

"The expression is, gag me with a spoon. Not a fork."

"Gag who with a spoon?" Adam asked.

"Sorry," I said with a sigh. "Just having a brief disagreement with Ruby about that saying."

"Do I want to know what she's referring to?"

I shook my head. "We should probably get going."

"Lead the way!" he said with a chuckle.

In the past month or so that we'd been hanging out together, he'd witnessed me having more than one disagreement with Ruby, and it seemed he'd become accustomed to hearing one-sided conversations. It used to fascinate him—he'd watch me with rapt attention and ask a million questions. But now, most of the time he simply let the conversation go.

I revved the engine and we took off, Ruby hollering in delight with Adam trailing me. He kept his distance so he didn't receive a face full of red dust, but followed close enough for me to hear his engine.

"Faster! Faster!" Ruby yelled, and I obliged. Okay, maybe she wasn't the only one who loved speed.

The handlebars shook in my grip as we bounced down the desert trail, buzzing by cacti and sagebrush toward the cliffs. Up ahead, the huge, red rock formations towered in the sky built by centuries of Mother Nature's infinite sculpting. I glanced behind me to find Adam lagging pretty far back.

"Dang, he's slow," Ruby said. "Where's his sense of adventure?"

"I'm sure he's riding at a speed he feels safe in."

"What's the fun in that? Half the excitement is the adrenaline of keeping the ATV righted and the fear of knowing you may crash."

I was about to argue, but quickly shut my mouth, a sinking feeling settling in my stomach. Shoot, she was right. I'd never considered it before, but that's what I also loved about riding ATVs and this suddenly bothered me. The rest of my life was led with careful planning and caution, except when I got on an ATV—a potentially dangerous activity that could get me killed.

Adam pulled up next to me and I smiled, determined to examine my supposed death wish later.

"You weren't kidding when you said you liked to ride!" he exclaimed. "You're fast, Bernie!"

"I should probably slow down. Sometimes I get a little out of control."

"Don't you dare!" Ruby said. "In fact, push this thing harder! I bet it's still got some juice we haven't used yet!"

"I was thinking we could stop over there." Adam pointed to the cliffs. "We should be able to see the moon come up. It'll be really spectacular."

And maybe a little romantic. Would I get my first kiss? "That sounds good. You can lead this time. I'll follow."

"Aw, Bernie," Ruby said when Adam went ahead. "Why are you letting him lead?"

"Because he's right. I'm going too fast and being dangerous."

"No, you aren't. Rule ten in life: don't let others take away your joy just because your definitions of happiness don't match. You like speed, he doesn't. And there's nothing wrong with either one."

"Except I could kill myself."

"Well, you haven't yet."

"It's a possibility."

"And you could die unloading the dishwasher. Jeez, Bernie. Don't fear death or you won't be able to live. Besides, it's not so bad."

I glanced over my shoulder at my grandmother, caught on this plane as a ghost, and I disagreed. I hated that she hadn't reached her final resting place and couldn't do all the things she used to love while alive. To me, her situation seemed downright awful.

"Okay, it's a little unpleasant," she said as if she read my mind.

I nodded and revved the engine, determined not to allow our conversation to sour my mood.

We rode for a good half hour at a normal speed. I found my mind wandering, thinking about upcoming reservations at the bed and breakfast, trying to recall if I had any milk left, and remembering the sheets I'd have to rewash after leaving them in the washing machine. A little boredom set in, but it was still nice to be out in the desert with Adam.

The sun sank behind the cliffs just as we arrived. At twilight, the desert became eerily quiet, the birds heading off to bed and the night critters waking from their slumber. Adam pulled off his backpack, unzipped it, and handed me a water.

"Thanks," I said, grabbing it and quickly drinking it down.

"I brought sandwiches as well." Sitting down on a rock, he pulled one out. "Peanut butter and jelly?"

"That sounds great." I took a seat next to him. "It's really thoughtful of you."

"I love peanut butter and I can't have any," Ruby

murmured as I took a bite of my sandwich. "I'm just going over here so I don't feel so sorry for myself."

An owl hooted nearby, then a few seconds later, silently flew right over our heads.

"That just about grazed my hair!" Adam said as we watched it take off into the distance.

"I know. Sometimes if I'm out after dark with Elvira, they try to get her." Elvira being my tabby who could stand to lose a few pounds.

"Seriously? She's a big cat."

"Yes, but I guess they get hungry and figure they can handle her."

"What does she do?"

"She's smart. She runs back inside."

"I thought she was just cranky?" Adam asked with a laugh.

"Smart and cranky."

He pulled out a flashlight and turned it on. "A deadly combination."

The light cast shadows all around us and I imagined javelinas and coyotes staring at us from deep within them, ready to strike when the time toast was right. The desert could be very dangerous at night, and Ruby had stories of being chased by the wild javelinas. I looked forward to the moon lighting our way home.

Ruby danced around about fifteen feet away. "I'm summoning the moon goddess!" she said in a loud, ecstatic voice.

A few minutes later, the moon peeked over the cliffs and lit up the whole area.

"Oh, wow," I said. "Isn't that gorgeous?" The moon appeared huge, as if it would swallow us up while bathing us in light.

"It is," Adam replied. "I'm so glad we came out."

For a few moments, we stood in awe observing the huge orb slowly ascending over the cliffs.

"Look up there!" Ruby said. "We can see those people!"

I glanced up, and indeed, two people were standing on top of one of the precipices. "Check it out," I said, pointing toward them and nudging Adam. "Do you think that's Jack's tour?"

"It may be," he replied.

One person left, leaving a lone figure who we could barely see standing far from the edge.

I turned to Adam. "Do you think we should head back? I worry about javelinas and stuff. Ruby told me some scary stories about being chased while out in the desert in the middle of the night."

He threw his head back and laughed. "Sure. Let's head out."

"Uh-oh," Ruby said.

I turned and found her staring up at the ledges. Following her gaze, I noted two silhouettes again, but this time, they were engaged in a scuffle.

"It's a fistfight!" Ruby yelled.

Why in the world would anyone be fighting on the edge of a cliff?

With a yell, one toppled over, plummeting hundreds of feet to the canyon below. I gasped and held back a scream. "Did you see that?" I whispered as the remaining figure stepped away from the ledge and out of our sightline.

Adam nodded. "Heck, yes. What the... I'm going to see if that guy somehow lived and call this in. Stay here until I get back."

After grabbing his helmet, he took off and I sat down again, unable to believe what I'd just witnessed.

"You okay, honey?" Ruby asked, squatting down in front of me. "You look paler than me."

I studied her ghostly form and I seemed to have developed a difficult time getting words from my head to my lips. My body trembled uncontrollably while ice had somehow replaced the blood in my veins. I rubbed my arms with my hands. When had it gotten so cold? "Did... did we just witness a m-murder?"

Ruby sighed and nodded, then pursed her lips together. "I think we did."

"T-there's no way that person could have lived through that f-fall."

"I agree," she said. "That tourist is toast."

CHAPTER THREE

A half-hour later, Adam returned. Ruby and I sat with my phone's flashlight on, and I became more frightened with each passing moment. Perhaps it was my past experience of being chased out into the desert at night, or I'd just suddenly developed a fear of the dark on top of my OCD and hatred of germs.

"I need to ride up there," Adam said. "It's Jack's tour. I talked to the office, and Jack called it in. I told them I was out here, and so I need to go secure the scene."

"Okay," I said, springing to my feet. "I'm assuming that man is dead?"

Adam sighed and closed his eyes for a moment. "Uh... yeah. I wish I could unsee that."

"We'll go with you," I said, buckling my helmet.

"It's not necessary," Adam replied. "Why don't you head home?"

Because I was afraid and didn't want to be alone. "I'd rather come with you, Adam," I said softly. "I'm not comfortable riding back by myself in the dark."

He stared at me a moment, then nodded. "It could be a late night."

"That's fine."

The joy from the evening had vanished, replaced by dread as we slowly made our way through the desert and up the trail leading to the cliffs. Even Ruby was quiet. When we reached the top, we found Jack leaning up against the Jeep, its headlights on and the motor running. Four people sat inside the vehicle, but I couldn't make out their features. The silence and sadness felt like an oppressive blanket.

"Hey," Jack said, his face pale and grim as he shook Adam's hand and nodded at me. "Thanks for coming out."

"Didn't have much of a choice." Adam pulled off his helmet. "Tell me what happened."

"This tour... it's been really difficult," Jack began. "There's been fighting and bickering. Even though all the people are in their fifties, they've been acting like a bunch of toddlers."

"Do they know each other?" Adam asked while

typing notes into his phone.

Jack shook his head. "They're two separate groups."

Adam furrowed his brow and glanced over Jack's shoulder at the people in the Jeep. "And they're fighting with each other?"

"Yeah." Jack shrugged. "It's been... crazy."

"Well, let's meet the children," Adam muttered.

I stuck close to Adam as Jack motioned them all into the headlights. Two women and two men. One of the women sniffled as if she'd been crying, while the second one had her arm wrapped around her shoulder, comforting her.

The two men stood stoically, their arms crossed over their chests.

"I'm Deputy Adam Gallagher," Adam said. "I'm sorry this evening has turned into such a nightmare."

"It was awful before that guy jumped," one of the men said.

Wait a minute. Jumped?

"No one jumped!" Ruby exclaimed. "He was pushed! We saw it, dummy!"

"What was the victim's name?" Adam asked.

"Harold," the crying woman said. "Harold Berg."

"And you are?" Adam asked.

She dabbed her eyes with a tissue. "His wife. My

name's Belinda." The slim, tall woman who seemed to be truly distraught, slurred her words. Was it grief, or had she been drinking?

"With a wife like her, I would have jumped, too," one of the men whispered to the other with a snicker.

Thankfully, Belinda didn't hear them.

"And your names?" Adam said, pointing at them.

"I'm Trevor, and he's Art."

Adam smiled at the woman comforting Belinda. "And you, ma'am?"

"Nancy," she said.

"Okay, now who is with who?"

"Belinda, Harold, and I are traveling together," Nancy said, then pointed at Trevor and Art with a sneer. "They aren't with us."

"Thank goodness," Art whispered.

Adam stared at the group for a moment, then glanced over at Jack. "Can I talk to you for a minute?"

The three of us—well, four of us, if I counted Ruby, which I probably should—stepped aside and gathered closely together.

"What the heck's up with these people?" Adam asked. "They all seem to hate each other."

"That's putting it mildly," Jack said, shaking his head. "Belinda, Nancy and Harold are all together.

For some reason, they thought they'd be taking the tour alone. Trevor and Art showed up, and they've been talking the whole trip. Finally, Belinda had enough and asked them to pipe down because she couldn't hear me. Trevor and Art said some horrible things, and then Harold got involved. It was like he just lost it. Like I said, I feel like I'm trying to placate a Jeep full of toddlers."

"What about Harold?" Adam asked. "What do you mean he lost it?"

"He was the worst." Jack's brows furrowed. "I hate speaking ill of the dead, but he was a nasty man. Awful to even Belinda and Nancy. I couldn't imagine being married to someone like him, but Belinda isn't any prize either."

Ruby and I traded glances. It had become abundantly clear that either we hadn't seen what we thought we had, or no one had any idea that Harold had been pushed to his death.

"Why does everyone think he jumped?" Ruby asked.

"Thanks, Jack," Adam said. "Can you please go stand over there with them?"

Adam grabbed my arm and turned us away from the others. "No one knows that Harold was murdered."

"I can see that."

"I'm going to go look for the place where Harold scuffled with his attacker. Do you want to go with me?"

"Sure. We'll do whatever we can to help, Adam."

"When can we go back to the hotel?" Belinda asked as we approached the group. Nancy still had her arm wrapped protectively around her friend. "I'm exhausted and it seems nothing is being accomplished with us standing out here all night. My wonderful Harold isn't coming back."

"We're waiting for the sheriff to arrive, ma'am," Adam said, his voice soft, but official. "I'm sorry for the wait, and for your loss. It won't be too much longer, and then we can get your statements."

As we walked away from the Jeep headlights, the moon lit our path. I stayed behind Adam as he treaded carefully, using the phone flashlight to search the ground.

"I think it was somewhere around here," he said.

"Nope. Farther up," Ruby replied, dancing along the edge of the cliffs. Her precarious position twisted my stomach, but it shouldn't. She was dead. And she'd jumped off a cliff before and bounced right back up, our tether not allowing her to go more than fifteen feet away from me.

"Ruby says it's up the path a bit," I said.

He nodded. "She's probably right. I can't find any signs of a struggle around here."

We walked a few more minutes with Ruby leading the way. "Here we go!" she yelled as she plunged over the edge. I gasped and shut my eyes despite the fact I knew she'd be fine.

A few seconds later, she reappeared on the ledge. "There are cars coming into the canyon. I can see their headlights."

I strained to attempt to glimpse over the side. "Ruby says this is where it happened. She says cars are coming."

"They're here to collect the body." Adam shone his flashlight around the dirt, and we easily found where the scuffle had taken place. At the edge, I could make out marks where someone's shoes had left skid marks.

He took a few pictures with his phone, then counted out steps as if he was measuring the area. I stood by quietly and allowed him to do his work.

"Can she see anything down there?" Adam asked.

"Who? Ruby?"

"Yes."

"Like what?"

His cheeks reddened even in the moonlight. "I don't know... like Harold's spirit?"

I glanced over at Ruby, who stood directly on the precipice. She shook her head. "I don't see any ghosts. But then again, I've proved that I'm not really a good ghost hunter."

"She doesn't see anything," I said, turning back to Adam.

"Okay." He let out a sigh. "I was hoping we could ask him who he fought with and who pushed him."

"Sorry, but I'm afraid not."

He turned back to his investigation as Ruby returned to my side. "Well, this night sure turned into a bummer."

"You're right."

"When do you think we'll be able to go home?" she asked.

I assumed I was free to leave whenever I wanted, but the thought of that ride in the dark, even with the moon illuminating from high above, gave me the creeps.

"Soon." I wasn't about to admit my anxiety to Ruby, who feared nothing.

"Not that I have anything better to do," she said with a snort. "But I find it interesting that no one here realizes that old Harold was murdered. Either one of them is lying or someone appeared out of nowhere and offed the guy."

I hadn't considered that the murderer could have been someone from outside the group.

"But at least you aren't a suspect in this one," Ruby continued. "We don't have to try to solve it. We can leave it to the professionals."

"You have a point," I murmured. "No one's coming after me."

Adam's phone rang, causing both Ruby and me to jump and screech. He glanced over his shoulder at me and shook his head as he answered.

"He's not so bad," Ruby said. "Even for a cop."

"I like him."

"Oh, I can see that," Ruby replied. "I noticed it the first time he showed up at our house when that guy was murdered upstairs." Adam continued studying the area and walking around while talking on his phone. "He also fills out those jeans nicely."

I sighed and rolled my eyes, even though she was right. Ruby cackled, always appreciating when she could get a bit of a reaction out of me.

Adam hung up the phone and strode over to us. "The sheriff is here. We need to head back to the Jeep."

"Aye-Aye, Captain!" Ruby said with a salute. "Lead the way!"

I fell in behind Adam with Ruby by my side, the trek back to the suspects seeming longer than when we'd left.

"What happened here?" Sheriff Bruce Walker asked, running a hand through his thick gray hair. In his seventies, he still possessed an intimidating glare as he pointed at me. "And why is she here?"

"We were out riding together, sir," Adam said. "As for what happened to Harold Berg, he was murdered."

"Well, hello, you old, cranky coot," Ruby scoffed, standing right next to the sheriff. "How's the most uptight man I've ever met?"

Walker narrowed his gaze as his nose twitched. He was probably catching a whiff of Ruby's distinct aroma—lavender and marijuana. "How do you know he was murdered?" he asked, then glanced back at the group. "Have they been smoking dope?"

Adam shook his head. "I'm not aware of any marijuana, sir. As far as the murder goes, we were down at the bottom of the cliffs. We saw two people in the moonlight. Then, one of them left. A few minutes later, two people started to fight and we actually saw the victim fall to his death."

"No kidding?"

"No, sir."

"Which one was it?" Walker asked, surveying the people there.

"We don't know," Adam said. "We could only make out silhouettes. We couldn't see any features."

"That's a darn shame. I guess we'll have to do this the old-fashioned way and investigate it."

"Yes, sir. They also seem to think that Harold jumped."

"How interesting. So one of them is lying."

"Unless there was an outsider around that we aren't aware of," Adam said. I noted his thought process followed Ruby's.

Ruby ghosted through the sheriff, causing him to shiver, and walked over to me. "Let's go home, Bernie. I can't stand being on the same cliff as that turd of a man."

Walker glanced around as if searching for something, probably thinking his mind was busy playing tricks on him. *Sorry, Sheriff. It's just Ruby.*

"Let's get everyone off the cliff," the man said. "We'll secure the area so we can investigate tomorrow. Jack can drive his Jeep. We'll put the tourists into the cop cars and everyone will meet down at the station. I want to get their statements tonight and give them orders they aren't to leave town."

Adam nodded and the two walked over to the group.

"Listen up!" the sheriff called. "Here's what's going to happen." I studied everyone as he shared his plan. One of them had killed a man not long ago, and the only one who seemed even mildly upset was Harold's wife, Belinda. I tried to match each person with the shapes that we'd seen up on the cliff, but none jumped out at me as being the murderer.

The group moaned and groaned when the sheriff finished. "Hey!" he yelled. "Y'all seem to think that Harold jumped to his death, but that's not the way it went down. I've got two witnesses who watched him being pushed. You are all now part of a murder investigation, so quit your whining!"

Everyone gasped and threw accusing glares at each other.

"He's kind of sexy when he gets riled up like that," Ruby said.

I personally didn't think there was anything sexy about the sheriff, so I didn't answer. Instead, I continued to study the suspects, looking for signs of guilt.

Who had pushed Harold?

CHAPTER FOUR

A moment of silence fell over the group. Belinda's eyes rolled to the back of her head as her knees gave out and she slid to the ground.

Nancy screamed and dropped next to her friend. Without thinking, I ran over with Ruby in tow and tried to make the poor woman comfortable by situating her head on her friend's lap.

"Are you all right?" I asked Belinda as our gazes met for a brief second. She shook her head and closed her eyes again. Tears streamed from the corners and fell onto Nancy's jeans.

"What does he mean we're in a murder investigation?" Nancy hissed. "Are you saying someone here killed Harold? How does the sheriff know?"

I glanced over my shoulder at the sheriff, then

turned back to her. Probably best to keep my mouth shut, but I felt she deserved an answer. "We were down in the canyon. We saw it happen."

Nancy stared at me a long while as if she couldn't quite understand what I was saying. With her short, brown pixie cut and sharp green eyes, she made for an attractive woman. "You *witnessed* his murder?"

"Yes."

"Oh, jeez, Bernie," Ruby said from behind me. "I hope she's not the killer. You may have just put a target on your back."

"Is she going to be okay?" the sheriff called.

"Do you think she needs medical help?" I asked.

"Belinda?" Nancy said softly. "Honey? Do you need a doctor?"

The woman shook her head. "I can't believe this," she whispered. "How did this vacation turn out to be so awful?"

I turned back to the sheriff. "She says she'll be fine."

"Now here's how this is going to work," Walker said. "You'll all get into a police car and we're taking you down to the station. There won't be any arguments about this. Your statements will be taken there." More moans and groans from the group. The sheriff pointed to me again. "You and Adam take the ATVs back into town with Jack and meet us at the station."

I looked at Adam and nodded. Apparently, I wouldn't be allowed to head home. It was going to be a long night.

"Gosh dang it!" Ruby yelled. "I hate the police station! I want to go home!"

I helped Belinda to her feet and watched everyone file into their assigned vehicles. The two police cruisers slowly pulled away, leaving Adam, Jack, Ruby and me alone.

"We better head back," Adam said.

Jack nodded. "I'll follow you two out."

After straddling the ATV, I slipped on my helmet with a long sigh. We drove slowly and carefully through the desert, a deep sadness and exhaustion settling in my chest. The fun of the ride had died long ago.

"Every time we come out on an ATV, something bad happens," Ruby said from behind me. "This sucks, Bernie."

I couldn't agree more.

I WAS ASKED to sit on a metal bench in the hallway right across from Belinda and Nancy. I noted red dirt marks on Belinda's white pants I hadn't seen before. Had she fallen or been in a scuffle while pushing her husband off a cliff? Or were they from her fainting spell?

Of course, Ruby was forced to join me and she complained about it, but because of my company, I couldn't tell her to stop. Instead, I just tried to tune her out, which was difficult at best. So, I concentrated on my rear end going numb from sitting on the hard surface for so long.

"I haven't been back here in a long while," Ruby said. "I can't remember what I was arrested for the last time, but old Bruce brought me into that interrogation room over there." She pointed at a closed door to Belinda's left.

Ruby's arrest record had been... interesting. Adam looked up her sheet once a few weeks back, and he found mostly petty crimes: smoking pot in public, one arrest for instigating a bar fight and another for public nudity. Ruby would never do anything to hurt someone, but she had enjoyed stirring the proverbial pot and living on her own terms.

"Shh," I whispered. Couldn't she see I was busy trying to eavesdrop on Belinda and Nancy?

The gunmetal paint and the matching tile on the floor gave me a headache, so I shut my eyes and leaned my head back on the wall, hoping I looked innocent and uninterested in their conversation.

"If he was killed, it had to be one of those men on the tour with us," Nancy said. "Remember they almost came to blows with Harold when we stopped on that overlook?"

"He was defending me," Belinda said, her words slurring. "They'd called me some awful names, which was unfair. I had only asked them to quiet down so I could hear what Jack was saying."

"I know, honey," Nancy whispered. "Harold loved you very much."

Belinda nodded. "We've had our issues, but yes. We did love each other."

Nancy sighed. "I don't have much faith in this sheriff, Belinda. He seems like an idiot."

I opened my eyes as Ruby shot to her feet. "Don't you dare call him an idiot! I'm the only one who gets to say that!"

"Well, hopefully he can find the killer," Belinda said, then broke into sobs once again. "My nose won't stop running. I need to use the restroom."

"I'll come with you," Nancy replied.

When they were out of earshot, I turned to Ruby. "Do you think she did it?"

"Which one?"

I shrugged. "Either."

"Heck, I don't know. What's their motive?"

"Well, Belinda said she and Harold had their problems."

Ruby sighed and sat down again. "Although I never married, it's my understanding that every couple has their issues. I always just walked away if my relationships ever entered the problem zone. Seemed easier than trying to ride it out. Life should be problem-free."

Figures. As for me, I'd never dated anyone long enough to make it to the problem zone, as Ruby put it. Belinda and Harold's issues had to be pretty big in order for murder to be the answer.

"And I'm warning you now, Bernie... if you date a cop, you'll have nothing but difficulties, no matter how charming he is or how good he looks in his jeans. I'm still standing by my recommendation not to date the police. This place is bringing back bad memories. Being cuffed is fun, as long as it's not in a police station."

Ruby rose and began to pace up and down the small hallway in front of me, as far as she could go.

We'd been in the hallway for hours and I was tempted to curl up on the bench to sleep. Even if I was released, I would have to walk home in the middle of the night. I didn't think I had the energy. I fought to keep my eyes open and my mind somewhat alert.

Sheriff Walker strode down the hall with a file folder in his hand and entered a room to my left without meeting my gaze. A second later, he poked out his head and glanced at the empty bench across from me.

"Where are they?" he asked.

"Bathroom."

He nodded and disappeared back inside the room. The two women returned a few moments later.

"Belinda Berg," the sheriff called. "Please join me in here." The two women headed for the door. "I need to talk to Belinda alone, Nancy."

The woman raised her chin and narrowed her gaze but remained quiet. Obviously, she didn't like the separation from her friend. When the door shut in her face, she shook her head and whispered a few curses, then walked back toward her bench, right through Ruby.

"Watch it, lady," Ruby muttered as Nancy

glanced around with her brow furrowed in confusion.

"Do you smell lavender?" she asked, meeting my gaze.

I shook my head and closed my eyes again.

We sat in silence for a few moments with Ruby continuing to pace.

"She's very wealthy, you know," Nancy said. "She'll have the best lawyer represent us and we'll be able to leave this dumpy town."

I opened one eye. No one had ever referred to Sedona as dumpy. In fact, with its majestic rock formations, the quaint town, and the beautiful surrounding desert, I would describe it as a precious gem.

"The only thing dumpy around here is your face, sweetheart," Ruby said.

I bit the inside of my cheek to keep from laughing.

"I'm going in here," Ruby said. I turned to see her ghosting through the door into where Belinda and the sheriff were talking. Even though I knew no one could see Ruby, it still startled me when she pulled moves like that. I immediately defaulted to thinking that she would be in trouble, and therefore, so would I.

"We should be in bed," Nancy said. "Belinda's had a horrible day. We all have."

"Tell me about it," I mumbled. I couldn't get the image of Harold falling to his death out of my mind.

Ruby had also made a really good point. I never should have admitted I was one of the witnesses who'd watched him die. What if the killer wanted to eliminate anyone who could finger them? I had no idea who the murderer was, but that didn't mean anyone would believe me.

Glancing at the door Ruby had gone through, I wondered what she was hearing. Hopefully she was listening and not trying to haunt the room. I'd have loved to be in there to eavesdrop on what Belinda had to say.

Nancy had mentioned Harold and Belinda were wealthy. Money was an excellent motive for murder.

A few moments later, Ruby reappeared and sat down next to me. "That woman is pretty full of herself," she said, hitching her thumb over her shoulder. "Says she's going to sue the sheriff for holding her here. She's a victim because she lost her husband."

I sat up and placed my elbows on my knees, my head in my hands. That way, Nancy couldn't see my face. "What else?" I whispered.

When I didn't get an answer, I glanced at the empty bench next to me. Ruby must have returned to the interrogation room because she was nowhere to be found. My attention was drawn to the footsteps coming down the hallway.

Adam.

He also carried a manilla folder. With a smile, he waved me into an interrogation room down the hall.

I stood and hurried over to him.

Ruby screamed from behind me, causing me to startle. I glanced over my shoulder to find her floating down the hallway on her back. "Bernie! She was just getting to the good part!"

"Sorry," I whispered, but kept walking toward Adam.

"This stupid tether!" Ruby yelled.

After Adam closed the door, he took me into a tight embrace. "How are you holding up?" he asked.

"Tired, but I'm fine." Dang, the hug felt nice. The tension in my shoulders faded as I leaned my head against his chest.

"Come sit down," he said, releasing me far too soon.

With a huff and a curse, Ruby stood in the corner.

I sat down as Adam pulled a piece of paper from the folder.

"I figured you must be exhausted, so I took the liberty of typing up a statement for you since we both witnessed the same thing. Read it over and let me know if you see any changes. If not, go ahead and sign it."

A little nig of discomfort wiggled in my belly. He was speaking for me? I didn't appreciate that one bit, but as I read the account, I realized just how exhausted I was and suddenly, I appreciated his efforts.

"It looks good to me," I said, grabbing the pen and scrawling my signature at the bottom.

"You didn't read that very carefully," Ruby said.

"It's fine," I replied, glancing over at her. Adam looked over his shoulder and waved.

"Ask him if we can go home," Ruby said. "I'm bored to tears."

I wanted to know what she had heard Belinda say to the sheriff, but I didn't think Adam would appreciate her sneaking around. The conversation would have to wait until we were alone.

"Bernie, I can't leave yet," Adam said. "Why don't you go to my house and stay there? Catch a few hours' sleep? It's right around the corner and you wouldn't have to walk home alone in the dark."

"We don't want to stay there," Ruby said. "No way, no how. That ghost threw a book at you!"

"He was aiming for *you*," I said, glaring pointedly at Ruby. "Maybe if you were a little nicer, he wouldn't feel the need to do such things."

Adam chuckled and sat back in his chair. "Is she afraid to stay at my house?"

"I'm not afraid of any ghost," Ruby said as she marched up to the table and stood right next to Adam. "That crazy guy hit my granddaughter with a book. She shouldn't subject herself to anymore abuse, copper."

"She's right next to me, isn't she?" Adam said. "I can smell her. And feel her. It's a little cold over here."

I nodded.

He turned to Ruby. "There hasn't been any para-normal activity at my place. I'm sure my ghost wouldn't mind you two visiting for a few hours... as long as you're nice."

It was the first time I'd seen him speak directly to her. Usually, he talked about her to me. Her eyes widened and she stepped away from him as if taken by surprise.

"I've got another couple hours of work here," he continued. "I'll bring home some coffee and bagels."

"He really believes I'm here," Ruby whispered, laying her hand over her heart. "He believes I exist."

"Yes, he does," I replied softly.

"Maybe he's not so bad after all."

Despite my exhaustion, I grinned.

"What did she say?" Adam asked.

"She said that we appreciate you offering your place and we promise to be nice to your ghost."

"I never said that!" Ruby yelled. "Quit putting words in my mouth, Bernie!"

"Great," Adam said, pulling the keys from his pocket and taking one off the ring. He slid it across the table. "Here you go. I'll see you in a little bit."

Ruby shook her head. "I can't protect you from that poltergeist, Bernie. You're making a huge mistake staying at Adam's place."

We'd be fine. Besides, poltergeist or not, I needed to sleep, and Adam's house offered me the shortest route to something besides a metal bench to do so.

And when I woke, I'd find out what Ruby heard in the exchange between Belinda and Sheriff Walker.

CHAPTER FIVE

Someone was watching me.

I had no idea how long I'd been asleep or where I was. But a scream tore from my throat when I opened my eyes and saw a bearded man wearing a cowboy hat standing over me.

Apparently, I had scared him as well because he also yelled and jumped away from me as I tried to untangle my legs from the blanket and stagger to my feet. Instead, my limbs remained snarled in the blanket and my shoulder hit the carpet with a loud thud.

"Why are you screaming like that?" the man shouted. "You're loud enough to wake the dead!"

I finally freed myself and rose to my feet just as Adam ran out into the living room trailed by Ruby, his gun at his side. "What's going on?" he asked, his gaze darting all around.

The sun shone brightly through the living room windows. What was the time? My breath sawed from my lungs while I ran a shaky hand over my hair. Staring at my bearded voyeur, I took in his faded jeans, the dingy white shirt with a huge bloodstain down the front, and cowboy boots. The deep lines on his face and the salt and pepper hair indicated he'd been probably in his sixties when he died. Adam's ghost.

"Well, well, well," Ruby said, her sights firmly set on the apparition. "Look who's finally decided to show himself."

"I don't want any trouble, ma'am," he said, holding his hands in front of him, as if that would stop Ruby from approaching. "I was simply wondering why the girl was sleeping on the couch. We don't see too many of the female persuasion in this here house."

Well, that was good news. "Because I was tired!" I said, rubbing my eyes. At least I knew Adam didn't have a string of women traipsing through his condo. "Why else would I be asleep?!"

"I could see you were snookered, like you'd had one too many tequilas," the ghost said, then hitched a thumb at Ruby. "How you rest with this one always talking, I have no idea."

"Oh! I love tequila!" Ruby squealed.

The ghost narrowed his gaze on me. "Why can you see me?" he asked. "I haven't been seen in decades."

I didn't possess enough energy to recite that story, so I ignored the question.

"Bernie," Adam said, still glancing around the room. "What's going on here? I feel like I'm missing out on a big conversation."

"You are," I replied. "I woke to your ghost standing over me."

Adam's eyes widened with surprise. "Seriously? You can see him? Did he try to hurt you?"

"I don't want to hurt no one," the visitor said.

Thank goodness. "Yes, I see him, and no, he doesn't want to hurt anyone."

"Don't you think it's time you introduce yourself, fella?" Ruby asked. "Or do we just make up a name for you? Maybe call you Old Coot Carl? Or Old Timer Tim?"

The ghost narrowed his gaze on Ruby. "Okay, Sea Hag Shirley." He then disappeared.

I dropped back on the couch and leaned my head against the cushion.

"Who is he?" Adam asked. "Why is he in my condo? What's he doing here?"

Ruby sighed and rolled her eyes. "Relax, copper. Give the girl a minute to catch her wits."

"He's gone, Adam," I muttered, still trying to wake fully.

"Are you okay, Bernie?" Adam sat next to me on the sofa and took my hand in his while he set down his gun. "Can I get you anything?"

"Did you bring coffee?" I asked.

"No. Canyon Coffee wasn't open yet when I came home. I'll make some."

"Thanks."

My heart calmed as I took some deep breaths and Adam hurried into the kitchen. I'd seen his ghost. Even though the apparition had thrown a book at me, he seemed fairly harmless—more curious than anything. As I recalled the meeting, I burst out laughing.

"Has anyone ever called you a sea hag before?" I asked, turning to Ruby.

Ruby lifted her chin trying to seem upset, but she also fought a smile. "No. I've been called a lot of things, but Sea Hag is a new one for me."

"He called her a sea hag?" Adam asked. Life would be so much easier if he could hear Ruby.

"Too bad he can't keep up," Ruby muttered, hitching her thumb over her shoulder toward the kitchen.

"Yes, he did," I replied to Adam. "After she called him an old coot and an old timer."

Adam sighed and shook his head while watching the coffee pot. "Ah. More name-calling. Wonderful. He's going to end up hating me. Did he say why he's here?"

I shook my head. "He seemed just as scared as me. He looked like some type of cowboy or miner. There was a huge bloodstain down the front of his shirt."

"You know what they say," Ruby said. "Save a horse... ride a cowboy instead." She hooted. I rolled my eyes and ignored her.

"Bloodstain!" Adam exclaimed. "Do you think he was shot or something?"

"That would be my guess. It looked awful." The blood had covered his chest down to his belly. "He had to have died that way. There was too much blood loss."

"Probably a cowboy from the old times," Ruby said. "Ran his mouth and got a bullet for his trouble."

As I stared at my ghost, relief swept through me that she hadn't been alive when shooting someone in the street was an okay thing to do. She wouldn't have lasted a day.

As Adam poured two cups and brought it over to me, the occurrences of the night before came flooding back. "What happened at the police station after I left?"

"I took Trevor White's statement, then I came home as well. I thought I'd be there a lot longer than I was."

"Can you tell me what he said?"

Adam shrugged. "It's an ongoing investigation, but I can give you the basics if you promise to keep it to yourself."

"Promise," I replied with a grin. I loved that he trusted me.

"Harold and his wife were jerks. The friend, Nancy, wasn't nice either. He described them as very self-important. At first, he thought they were some kind of celebrities because they said they were from Los Angeles, but quickly decided they were just rude."

I took a long gulp of the hot liquid. "This tastes amazing, Adam. Thank you."

"Sure. I should have asked if you needed cream or sugar."

"No, this is perfect. Where is Trevor from?"

"He and Art are from the Seattle area—a place north of the city called Everett."

"What are they doing here?"

"It rains a lot in Seattle. They're golfing buddies here for the weather. They spent a few days down in Phoenix, then came up to see the wonders of Sedona."

"What did Art have to say?"

Adam yawned and stretched his hands over his head. "I don't know. The sheriff interviewed him and I haven't read the file."

We sat in silence for a long moment. Harold may have been killed by one of those people who had ridden on that Jeep tour and I longed to know which one had done it. But what if the killer was someone else on that cliff? Someone no one knew was there?

"Did Jack give any other hints on who he thinks pushed Harold?" I asked.

Adam pursed his lips and shook his head. "No. In fact, he clammed up and said he wanted a lawyer."

"That makes him look guilty," I said.

"Tell me about it."

"I'm a little surprised by him," I said. "I would think he'd want to put the horrible night behind him, not draw it out with more interviews and getting a lawyer involved."

"Mr. Dimples didn't kill anyone," Ruby said with a huff. "He's too cute to be a killer."

"Anyway," Adam continued, "I need to get back to the station. "Belinda called her lawyer and we were hoping to talk to her again before he arrives and muzzles her."

My phone dinged and I grabbed it from the coffee table. The screen indicated someone had made a reservation and would be checking in shortly. "Looks like I've got a customer coming."

"We've both got busy days," Adam said.

"Yes, we do." I stood and downed the rest of my coffee in one large gulp. "I'll see you later. Call me and keep me posted on the case."

"I will."

As I hurried home with Ruby at my side, I made a mental list of things I needed to do before my guests checked in. The rooms should be ready for visitors, but I'd better double-check them in case I missed anything on the first cleaning. The living room should also get a quick dusting, and I wanted a shower. Elvira, my cat, would need to be fed, and I should see whether I needed milk and sugar for coffee in the morning. If I did, a quick jaunt to the grocery store would be in order.

"Who's coming to visit?" Ruby asked as she skipped down the sidewalk next to me. "Anyone interesting?"

"Two women from Phoenix," I said. "One is getting married and looking at wedding venues in Sedona."

"Oh! How fun," Ruby replied. "Be nice to them and maybe we can score an invite. I do love a good Macarena dance."

"I thought you hated the idea of marriage," I said, glancing over at her while she twirled down the sidewalk, the purple mumu flaring around her calves.

"For me, I do. Or I did, I should say. I'm not marriage material. Never was."

Wasn't that the truth. I appreciated the fact she admitted it and never tried to force herself to be something she wasn't while alive. Ruby may be difficult at times, but she was always unashamedly honest with herself and others.

"Adam's ghost is sure... unusual," she said.

"With the way you've been badgering him, I'm surprised he showed himself."

Ruby chuckled and spun around in a circle.

"Well, being nice wasn't exactly working. I wonder what Old Coot Carl's story is."

"Maybe if you're nice, he'll tell us. And that begins by you quitting with the nicknames."

"We'll see," she replied with a shrug.

She remained uncharacteristically quiet for a block, and I wondered if thoughts of the ghost occupied her mind. For the first time, she'd met someone like her who hadn't passed on to their resting place. Why had both of them been trapped on this plane after their demise?

"So who do you think pushed the old guy off the cliff?" Ruby asked.

"He was what... twenty years younger than you?" I replied with a snicker.

"Whatever. Who do you think did it?"

"I don't know, Ruby. I haven't given it much thought. It's not really my place to figure that out."

"Aren't you curious?"

"Sure I am. Adam and Sheriff Walker will find out who did it, and then we'll know. You never told me what you heard in the interrogation room between Sheriff Walker and Belinda."

We rounded the corner and my house came into view.

"It wasn't much," Ruby said. "She was obviously

pretty distraught, but something didn't seem right to me. I was thinking about it all night, but I can't place my finger on it. I'll give you the details after your guests arrive."

"Why not now?"

"Because I can feel your anxiety ramping up just walking next to you. It's so strong, if I had a heart, it would be beating too fast. I'm sure you have a long list of stuff you want to do before they get here."

I almost argued, hating that I was so transparent, but also appreciating that she knew me so well and respected my processes.

Still, I had to do a better job controlling my anxiety. I never realized how bad it was until I could see Ruby. With her always pointing it out, I was beginning to see that I very well may have a problem I never even realized I had. With all my exercise and eating right, I had always considered myself healthy, but maybe I wasn't. Stress could do awful things to a body.

"You're right," I said. "I do have a list, but I want to find out what you overheard once everything is settled.

"Ten-four, Danno."

Just as I shut the panel to my cleaning supply closet, the bell on the front door jingled, indicating someone had entered.

"Oh, this is so pretty!"

"It really is. I'm glad we decided to stay here instead of a hotel."

With a smile, I rounded the corner to greet my guests. "Hey! I'm Bernadette, the owner." I stuck my hand out and shook theirs, pegging them both in their mid-twenties.

"We love the living room," the blonde with long hair said as she gazed all around.

"Thank you." Two high-backed flowered couches sat facing each other, providing a pathway to the large wooden fireplace. I'd lined up the cushions and throw pillows with precision, and the huge chandelier hung from the ceiling right between them. With the natural light coming in through the windows, I had to admit, it was a stunning room. "I hope you like the rest of the house just as well."

After leading them over to the little desk in the corner, I took down their information and charged their credit card. "I understand you're looking at wedding venues?"

"Yes!" Amy, the exuberant blonde, said. Pegging her as one of those people who became excited about everything, I also guessed she did the talking for the both of them, because I'd gotten nothing from her friend Cathy but a brief smile. "I'm the one getting married and I'm very spiritual. I'm considering an outdoor wedding at one of the vortexes. I want the energy to bless our union."

Sedona was famous for its energy vortexes and many people believed them to be helpful to healing, self-exploration, and meditation.

Ruby snorted as she appeared behind the two women. Even though she'd spent most of her adult life in Sedona, she didn't believe in the vortex energy so many came to experience.

"When's the ceremony?" I asked.

"I'd like to be married at the beginning of fall,

when the weather isn't too hot but not cold yet, either."

"I'm sure you'll find somewhere lovely to hold your ceremony," I replied. "That time of year is really pretty. Jack over at Jumping Jack Jeep Tours may be able to help you out by driving you around. He's got a whole list of beautiful places to show you."

Amy and Cathy exchanged glances. "Oh, my gosh!" Amy shrieked. "That would be amazing!"

"You'll find a brochure in your room, so you can call and make a reservation. Tell him what you're looking for, and I'm sure he'll be able to help you out."

"What about breakfast?" Amy asked. "Is one served? We saw some reviews about how good it was."

Darla Darling, who owned Darling's Diner, used to provide breakfast for my guests. But, she was no longer my friend because of a huge misunderstanding and her own insecurities. Since we were no longer on speaking terms and a drunk monkey had better culinary skills than me, I'd taken breakfast off my list of amenities.

"We'll have donuts and coffee," I replied.

"Oh, that won't do. Sugar goes straight to my thighs. I have to fit into a wedding dress!"

At least I didn't have to buy donuts. "If you're watching your calories, then I would suggest a smoothy from Sarah's Smoothies in town. They're very filling and if you choose the right one, they're also healthy."

"If you're a cow," Ruby said. "Lemongrass, wheatgrass, barley... all cow food."

"I enjoy the lemongrass and blueberry with extra probiotics," I said, smiling. "It's one of my favorites." Besides the chocolate and peanut butter with mounds of whipped cream, but I'd keep that little secret to myself.

"It does sound wonderful," Amy agreed. "We'll definitely have to give it a try."

Cathy cleared her throat. "I read online that this place is haunted."

My gaze slid over to my resident ghost who stood right behind Cathy, smiling and rubbing her hands together as if she couldn't wait for the haunting to begin. "Some people have experienced strange things," I replied. "But others haven't."

Cathy leaned her forearms onto the desk. "I'd appreciate it if I didn't experience anything but a good night's sleep."

A stunning woman with a black pixie cut and blue eyes, her gaze held a hint of fear. Glancing over at Ruby again, who had broken out into a song about marriage equating a ball and chain, I couldn't make any promises.

"I'm sure you'll be fine," I replied. "The most anyone has reported is strange odors. Nothing beyond that."

"Boo!" Ruby yelled right in Cathy's face, then cackled.

Cathy narrowed her gaze. "I think I smell... lavender? And something else? What is that, Amy?"

"I'm not sure," Amy replied, sniffing the air.

"Is this some type of joke?" Cathy asked. "I mean, I mention a ghost and now weird odors are floating around?"

"Relax. It's probably just your imagination," the bride-to-be said. "There's no such thing as ghosts."

Oh, how I wished she was right. My resident apparition waved her arms in the air and rolled her eyes in the back of her head while groaning, her meager attempt at scary sorely lacking.

"Well, here are your keys," I said, handing one to each of them. "Your rooms are up the stairs on the left side." Since I only had king beds, the women had requested separate sleeping quarters.

"Great," Amy said. "We appreciate it."

"I hope you enjoy your visit. Let me know if I can do anything for you."

As they waved and made their way up the stairs, Ruby thankfully stayed with me. "Please leave them alone tonight," I whispered. "Cathy doesn't want to have any paranormal experiences."

"She's no fun."

"Promise me you'll leave them alone?"

"Fine," Ruby said with a huff. "I promise. Why does your place attract such boring guests?"

I didn't bother to answer and instead walked into my room where I grabbed a load of laundry, then into the laundry room where I shoved it into the washer. When the washing machine hummed along, I returned to the bedroom to find Ruby sprawled out on the yellow comforter with my tabby cat, Elvira, who tended to be a little moody except when with my grandmother.

After shutting the door, I took a seat on the rocking chair by the window wishing I had brought in a glass of water. "Tell me what you heard while you were spying in the sheriff's office."

"Mr. Dimples wasn't lying when he said Belinda was a piece of work."

"What did Sheriff Walker have to say about it?"

Ruby sighed, her forehead pinched in concentration. "Well, she demanded he allow her to return to her hotel—that one fancy place that reminds me of a mausoleum. I don't remember the name of it, but I'd never stay there. Too uptight for me. Old Bruce told her she'd have to wait until he was done interviewing her. Now, knowing Bruce the way I do, I bet that if she hadn't been such a hoity-toity snot, he would've let her go and caught up with her the next morning. But she pushed him and became more and more haughty, and he responded in kind."

"Interesting. Sounds like it was a war of wills rather than an interview."

"Yes, I'd say so—a regular one-upmanship, or a power play. Belinda, Harold, and their friend Nancy were all staying together. Nancy's a friend of the family."

"Staying together? As in the same room?"

"Yeppers. Made me wonder if there wasn't a little funny business going on between the three of them."

I stared out the window. How strange was it that three adults, two married and one single, shared one room? It had never happened in my bed and breakfast, but I suppose people could travel that way and most likely did.

"She kept going on about how much money she

had," Ruby continued. "Said she'd buy and sell the sheriff and he'd be in big trouble if he didn't take his focus off her and Nancy."

"What did he say to that?" I couldn't imagine he appreciated her efforts in pushing him around.

"Bruce told her money was the perfect motive and he had to investigate everyone involved in the crime, and that included her because he assumed she would be the beneficiary of the estate."

"That makes sense."

"Sure it does. Wife offs the annoying husband and can spend the money any way she wants. If I were ever married to a rich guy who irritated me, I'd consider it."

"You would not."

Ruby shrugged and giggled. "Maybe or maybe not."

The problem with her theory was she would have to agree to marriage in the first place, something she'd never done.

"If Belinda and Harold are so rich, why are the three of them sharing a room?" I asked. "Why not reserve a separate room for Nancy?"

"Good question. Perhaps no one likes privacy. Maybe Harold's a tightwad and he'd rather have

Nancy around all the time instead of spending the extra money."

I would think the married couple would want solitude, but perhaps I was wrong. Either that, or Ruby was correct and there was some funny business going on between the three of them, which was also none of my concern.

"Did she give any indication on who pushed him?" I asked.

"She said that obviously it was one of the two men in their group because Nancy was her best friend and would never cause her any pain. Then you pulled me out of there."

I recalled how shielding Nancy had been of her friend, both on the cliff and in the sheriff's office. She'd even tried to accompany Belinda into her interview with the sheriff, almost as if Belinda was incapable of speaking for herself.

"In my intelligent opinion, Nancy is acting like Belinda's watchdog," Ruby said. "I understand wanting to help a friend, but she seemed... maybe overprotective?"

"I agree, Ruby. There's something different about their relationship."

Darla and I had been close—probably the closest friend I'd ever had. But I couldn't picture either one of us hovering over each other the way Nancy had with Belinda. Some days I truly missed Darla and I became a little teary. But then I recalled how crazy she'd become and how hurtful she'd been, and I got over it darn quick. It would take a miracle to repair the damaged relationship.

"For the record, that woman had been drinking," Ruby said. "Not that it's a big deal, but she was slurring her words a little bit."

"That's interesting," I replied. "I didn't think Jack allowed alcohol on his tours for liability reasons."

"Maybe she carries a flask. The best of us do. And speaking of Jack... what do you think about Mr. Dimples getting a lawyer?"

"Jack? Well, I can't see him going from Jeep tour operator to murderer, but it does seem strange to me. Maybe he lost his cool with all the fighting and pushed Harold. I don't know."

A knock sounded at my bedroom door and Ruby and I exchanged glances.

I rose from the chair and opened the panel to find Amy and Cathy. Both looked somewhat uncomfortable as they shuffled their weight from one foot to the other and Cathy wouldn't meet my gaze.

"What can I do for you?" I asked, wondering

how long they'd been standing there and if they'd been listening.

"Well, we're leaving," Amy said. "We wanted to let you know."

"Um... thank you, but you don't have to tell me when you're coming and going." Mental note: include this bit of information in the check-in speech from now on.

Amy glanced over my shoulder, searching for someone or something. "Okay, we weren't sure," she said. "We've never stayed at a bed and breakfast before."

"If you're going to be out past ten, you can phone me," I replied. "I can give you instructions on how to enter the house once the doors are locked."

"Great. Thanks."

Neither moved.

"I... I need to get back to my phone call," I said. "Is there anything else?"

Amy didn't bother to try to hide her surprise or confusion. She stared at me with wide eyes, her mouth in a perfect O, and I couldn't figure out why. Didn't she believe my lie? "No," she whispered. "We'll see you later."

I waited until the bells chimed on the front door,

then shook my head and turned to Ruby. "How much do you think they heard?"

Ruby shrugged. "I have no idea. Nice move telling them you were on the phone instead of chatting it up with your dead grandma."

"Thanks," I muttered, running a hand through my hair. I'd never had a guest invade my private space like Cathy and Amy had, and even though they hadn't stepped in the room, the space suddenly felt violated.

"You've only got one problem," Ruby said.

"What's that?"

"Your phone's on the kitchen counter."

After glancing around at all the regular surfaces I usually left the device on, I hurried out to the kitchen. On the pristine, uncluttered counter sat my phone. They'd have to be blind not to see it.

"Maybe they thought I have two phones."

Ruby sauntered out of my bedroom, chuckling. "Or perhaps they thought you were talking to your resident scary ghost."

With a groan, I shut my eyes. Not only did my guests probably think I was crazy sitting in a bedroom talking to myself, they also might have overheard the gossip about the murder. Hopefully, they wouldn't repeat any of it while in town.

The last thing I needed was more people hating me. I'd already been the town pariah once before, and thankfully, that had died down. I didn't want to become the target of loathing again. This time, they may run me out.

CHAPTER SEVEN

The next morning, I had coffee with Amy and Cathy in the living room. The spring morning held a bit of a chill, so I lit the fireplace and the flames quickly warmed the room. Ruby had yet to show herself and Elvira hid under my bed.

"Did you get to explore a little yesterday?" I asked the women as I sipped cinnamon brew with cream from my mug. It wasn't as delicious as the goodness from Canyon Coffee, but it did the job and tasted decent.

Amy smiled and nodded. "A little bit. I love the stores here... We did some shopping."

"Oh, good! Where did you go?"

"Our first stop was Sarah's Smoothies and we

each had the Lemongrass and Blueberry drink you recommended. It was tasty and very energizing."

"Then we went over to Elizabeth's Essentials," Cathy chimed in, surprising me. "She showed us a wonderful lavender oil mix that helps with sleep. I tried it last night, and I can't remember the last time I've rested so well. A couple of dabs to my temples and to the bottom of my feet and I was out."

Maybe that was why Cathy wasn't overly chatty—she simply needed a decent eight hours. Or perhaps she was one of those people who remained quiet until she really knew a person and felt comfortable around them.

"I also picked up a purse at Boots and Bags," Amy said. "A cute little red and yellow leather one. It reminds me of springtime."

The bag she spoke of had been sitting in the window for a few weeks, and it had caught my eye as well. Since the owner, Michael, hand-stitched all his wares, it would be considered a one-of-a-kind as no two of his items were ever the same.

"I love that purse," I said, now disappointed I hadn't picked it up for myself. "He does amazing work."

We chatted for a few more moments about the

other items the women noticed in the store, then I asked, "Did you schedule a tour with Jack?"

Amy and Cathy exchanged glances, shaking their heads. "We were uneasy about doing that," Amy replied.

"How come?" Although, I had a pretty good idea why. They'd heard everything I'd said the prior day while talking to my ghost.

"Well, we read in the paper that he may be involved in a murder and we didn't feel comfortable having him take us out, especially to secluded areas."

I hadn't checked the paper in the past couple of days, so I couldn't verify if Jack had been mentioned in the reporting. If he had been, that would definitely hurt his business. In a way, I hoped Amy and Cathy were being truthful and they hadn't overheard me.

"We better get going," Cathy said. "We're heading out to two of the vortexes today to scout the area."

"Which ones?"

"Cathedral Rock and Bell Rock."

The two were the most popular, although Sedona was said to hold many others—a truly spiritual and magical place.

"Do you need more information on them?" I asked. "They each have very different energies."

Amy nodded and set down her cup. "Sure!"

They listened intently as I gave my quick spiel I had recited many times: Cathedral Rock was a magnetic vortex full of yin, or feminine energy, while Bell Rock consisted more of masculine energy. "Honestly, for a wedding, I think Cathedral Rock would be a better place. The energy is more soothing, more maternal."

"That's great to know," Amy said. "Thanks for the tips! I'll see how I feel at each one."

"And remember, the vortexes will augment your moods and make them more pronounced," I continued. "If you're happy while there, you'll experience a blissful state. If you're unhappy, you'll only feel worse."

Amy turned to Cathy. "You better put a smile on your face and think cheerful thoughts."

"Right?" Cathy said with a laugh. "Like I need to be any crankier."

At least she knew her disposition wasn't the best.

"Have a fun time," I said, walking them to the front door. "And please reconsider booking Jack. He's a personal friend of mine and I know he didn't have anything to do with murdering anyone."

At least, I hoped not. It would be creepy having a friend who's a killer.

No sooner had they left and I poured another cup of coffee, the door chimes rang again. Imagine my surprise when I ventured into the entryway and found Darla Darling standing there, her arms crossed over her chest, her brow furrowed in anger. With her leggings, tank top, and the beads of sweat dotting her brow, I guessed she'd been out on a run and decided to drop by unannounced, something she hated when others did the same to her.

"Hi, Darla," I said, frozen in place. She was the last person I ever expected to see. "What can I do for you?"

"I wanted to talk to you about Jack," she replied.

"Okay," I said, sighing. Jack had been the reason Darla and I were no longer friends. Unbeknownst to me, she'd begun dating the biggest womanizer in Sedona and thought I also wanted a piece of him, which simply wasn't true. Jack and I were friends, and I had no desire to get tangled up with him. The whole argument had been unfair, silly, and childish. Frankly, I still didn't fully understand it.

I sat on one sofa, and she lowered herself on the other. As she glanced around the room and arranged the throw pillows behind her back, I took a couple of deep breaths and braced myself for the chat.

Finally, she met my gaze and tucked a lock of

blonde hair behind her ear. "Two women were in my diner yesterday. I overheard them discussing Jack's involvement in that man's murder."

As I sipped my coffee, I hoped my features remained neutral. Unfortunately, my feelings for any situation were usually written all over my face, whether I wanted them there or not. "And?"

"You were the source for the information, Bernie."

"They told you that?"

"I overheard it."

Ruby appeared behind Darla and smiled. "Look who it is. The most boring girl in Sedona. What's she doing here?"

Pursing my lips together, I tried not to smile. Ruby had never liked Darla and never failed to make her feelings clear. It used to bother me, but now I just found her a little amusing.

"Bernie?" Darla asked. "What do you have to say for yourself?"

"Well, first, I have no idea who you're talking about." *Liar, probably your guests.* "Second, there is a constitutional amendment allowing me to say just about anything I want. And third, perhaps you should quit eavesdropping on your customers' conversations and mind your own business."

I smiled sweetly while Ruby clapped. "That's my girl!" she yelled. "Don't let this yahoo push you around!"

Darla's face turned apple-red. "Why are you doing this to me?"

I stared at my former friend, confused beyond belief. "What do you mean? What am I doing to you?"

She shook her head. "You want to poison my relationship with Jack."

I set down my coffee cup on a side table and tried to keep my cool. "Darla, I'm not poisoning anything. What you do in your life is your business. I couldn't care less about your relationship with Jack. In fact, I wish you both nothing but happiness. I'm not trying to come between you two. I'm not trying to cause a breakup."

"You told the police that I was involved in the last murder this town had. Remember? The guy who died in *your* upstairs bedroom? And then you tried to date Jack behind my back."

"I've never tried to date Jack," I said through gritted teeth, now highly annoyed and unable to hide it. How I wished I didn't allow her to rile me. "And as far as Mr. Gonzalez's death, you were a key part of that investigation because you were involved. You were a witness to what happened leading up to the crime. What was I supposed to do?"

"Keep me out of it!" she yelled. "And keep Jack out of it as well! Maybe you're the one the police should be investigating since you seem to turn up at every murder!"

Her chest heaved as her eyes widened, her fists clenched in her lap. I barely recognized her. Darla and I had been close. We'd enjoyed the same things. Now, I couldn't understand where the paranoia stemmed from and why.

"This one is nuttier than a squirrel turd," Ruby said, shaking her head. "Get her out of here, Bernie. Who knows what she's capable of? Right now, she looks like she may blow her top."

"Listen to me, Darla," I said, trying to keep my voice even. "Jack was at the murder site. Do I think he had anything to do with it? Certainly not. However, the police are going to investigate him simply because he was there. It's a fact."

"That doesn't mean you have to tell your guests about it!"

There was no way to tell her that I wasn't speaking to my customers, but to my ghost. "They overheard me on the phone," I replied. "I'd never spread rumors on purpose."

"Oh, please," Darla spat. "Give me a break, Bernie. Of course you would. You have in the past, so why should the present be any different?"

"How... when have I spread rumors in the past?" I asked, now more perplexed than ever.

Darla rolled her eyes as if I were the dumbest person on the planet. "When you told the cops about my involvement with Mr. Gonzalez's murder! What is wrong with you?!"

Hadn't I just explained exactly why I needed to give her name to the police? I rubbed my face and sighed. Any logic that had been in this room had flown right out the window. Ruby was right. Darla needed to leave.

"Listen, Darla. Here's the actual truth. First, I'm not trying to involve you or Jack in anything. I'm sorry those two women overheard me talking. I'm sorry you eavesdropped on their conversation and your mind has spun this... this conspiracy theory, for lack of a better term."

Her eye began twitching and her face reddened further. I actually worried for her health. "Are you okay?"

"Shut up, Bernie," she hissed. "I see you for what you are. You're like a pretty snake lying in the grass waiting to strike. You open your mouth and spit venom, poisoning everything in sight. You smile and flip your ponytail all innocent like, but then your ugly side comes out."

She stood and marched to the front door, leaving me speechless. When the panel slammed, the foundation of the house seemed to vibrate, along with my self-esteem. A small part of me wondered if she wasn't the only one who saw me in such a light. Did I deserve this? I didn't think so, but dang it, did her tirade hurt.

"My goodness," Ruby muttered. "What's gotten into her?"

"I honestly don't know," I replied, shaken to my core. "She's not herself."

"She wins in the paranoia department. And what was that snake nonsense? That barely made any sense."

As I stared at the closed door, I couldn't help but feel that Darla had some serious issues. Her illogical suspicions of me hurt, but it seemed to come from a dark place where everyone was out to get her. Or, at least, in her mind, I was. What twas going on in her life? Did she need medical attention? Darla had upset me greatly, but deep down when I pushed past the achy loss of our friendship, I still cared for her.

Perhaps I was overstepping my boundaries, but

the idea that Darla needed help sat firmly in my mind.

Without her having any family in town, I struggled with who I should approach. Who cared for her? Who would she listen to?

Only one person came to mind.

CHAPTER EIGHT

"I simply can't believe you want to go see Mr. Dimples without me," Ruby pouted. "It's a tragedy right up there with plane crashes and Janis Joplin dying."

"Ruby, I'm sorry," I said with a sigh as I pulled on my red *Back to the Future* T-shirt and a black sweater. "I need to have a serious conversation with Jack, and frankly, it's hard to do when you're around. I can't concentrate with you admiring the way his jeans fit."

"What if I promise to keep quiet?"

I glanced over my shoulder at her lying on the bed. As she met my stare, we both burst out laughing.

"Okay, okay," she said. "I get it. I'll stay here with Elvira."

"Thank you. I would love for you to tag along, but I need to be able to focus. Darla's health is a delicate subject." And so was murder. The fact Jack had lawyered up still bothered me and I wanted to ask him about it. A series of very important conversations, indeed.

I checked my reflection one last time before I left. Although I wasn't interested in Jack, I did want to look presentable. After I ran a comb through my long black hair, I added a little balm to my dry lips.

"Give your cheeks a little pinch as well," Ruby called from the bedroom. "You need some sun."

"I'm not going out in the sun," I muttered, then applied a quick swipe of blush.

"Tell Mr. Dimples I said hello, and snap a picture of that cute butt of his," Ruby added as I strode out.

Instead of walking, I drove, although I could've used the exercise. I still hadn't decided if Ruby was a good or bad influence on me. One day I appreciated her love of life and living in the moment, the next I wondered if my own existence was slowly spinning out of control. I'd put on a few pounds and didn't exercise nearly as much as I used to. Instead, I drank chocolate and peanut butter smoothies and watched reruns of Tom Selleck as *Magnum PI* with my dead grandmother. I even found myself gushing about him right along with her.

When I pulled into Jack's parking lot, I glanced over at the diner. If Darla was there and happened to peek out the window, she'd be furious I had stepped foot at Jumping Jack's Jeep Tours. For a second, I debated whether to leave. Perhaps I was sticking my nose where it didn't belong. Was Darla's health and the fact Jack had hired a lawyer really any of my business?

"Probably not," I muttered, throwing the SUV into reverse. Just as I was about to back out, Jack emerged from his office and waved at me. Did I go and come up with an excuse later, or did I try to help Darla and find out what Jack was thinking?

With a curse, I turned off the engine and emerged from the car.

"Hey!" he greeted me, smiling.

"Hi, Jack." I approached him. Despite his grin, I noted the usual shimmer in his green gaze had fizzled. In fact, deep purple circles hung under his eyes and his coloring resembled a ghost's. Was it illness, stress over Darla, or guilt from killing a man? "I was wondering if you had a few minutes to talk."

"Sure. I'm pretty slow today. Come on in."

I followed him into the small, no-frills office. He sat behind the desk, then I took my place on the other side and inhaled deeply. Serious conversations caused my nerves to rattle and I wiped my sweaty palms on my jeans.

"What's up?" he asked, folding his hands across his stomach.

Gosh. Where did I begin? The murder or the meltdown?

"Adam told me you hired a lawyer," I blurted. Apparently for me, discussing death was easier than talking about someone's mental health. "I was wondering why."

His easy smile faded and he pursed his lips. Finally, he said, "I just felt I'd be better off with a lawyer. I was there and didn't want to be accused of the killing. A lawyer gives me a layer of protection."

"But you didn't have anything to do with Harold's death, right?"

Jack shook his head. "I didn't, but between you and me, I thought about it. The man was rude. Told me I'd never amount to anything driving Jeeps in the desert, that I was a loser."

I gasped, surprised by the level of jerkiness some people stooped to. "Seriously?"

"Oh, yeah. He was a moron to everyone, except his wife, Belinda. Well, even then, he was just *less* of a jerk."

"In other words, a real prize of a human being."

"Exactly." Jack's gaze flitted all around the office as if trying to find an answer to an unasked question, or even weighing how much to tell me. "You know, I've had some bad experiences in my past. I've done things I'm not proud of, things I want to stay hidden."

I remained still, trying to decipher what he meant. Was he about to confess he *had* actually pushed Harold? Was that what shamed him? I held my breath.

"When I came to Sedona, I wanted a fresh start," he continued. "I didn't want my past to haunt me so I've been very careful about who to trust and what to say. That's why I got the lawyer."

"What happened, Jack?"

He shook his head. "I made mistakes, Bernie. Bad decisions. Right now, I'm a respectable citizen of Sedona and I don't want that to change. I don't need the police digging into my past, looking for reasons to pin the murder on me."

My goodness. What in the world could he have done to make the police think that? "A lawyer isn't going to stop them from looking at you," I said. "To me, the fact you hired one makes you look guilty."

Jack chuckled and shook his head. "You're probably right, but what can I say? I panicked. I was up on the cliff looking at the beautiful moon, literally wishing Harold would fall to his death. I fantasized about pushing him. Then, I did a headcount and realized he was missing. After searching everywhere, we couldn't find him, so I called it in. The next thing I knew, Adam was announcing I was in the middle of a murder investigation."

"Yeah, it's a little jarring when you find yourself in that situation."

"You know exactly what I'm talking about," he said, sighing. "I've been in trouble before, Bernie. I don't want any trouble again, so I did the only thing I could think of."

"I don't blame you. I understand. It's a sickening feeling." I recalled when I'd been thrust into Mr. Gonzalez's murder investigation, and it still cramped my stomach and caused my breath to hitch.

"A lawyer isn't going to do me much good, and I realize that," Jack said. "At the time, it seemed like the smart thing to do. At least he'll stop me from saying anything stupid to the police that would cause me to implicate myself."

We sat in silence for a moment while I wondered what was hidden in Jack's proverbial closet.

Jack broke the ice. "I'm glad you showed up. I've actually got a bone to pick with you."

"What's that?" As I asked the question, I figured I could guess what he wanted to talk about.

"Darla told me you were gossiping about me." The smile indicated he wasn't upset. Perhaps curious?

I shook my head. "I wasn't. I was on the phone with... with a family member and I was telling them about that night. I may or may not have mentioned you were there and you'd be considered a suspect and that you'd hired a lawyer. I wasn't telling anyone you killed Harold." Well, perhaps I had. *Maybe he lost his cool with all the fighting and pushed Harold.* I squirmed in my seat, recalling the words.

"Ah. She made it sound like you were running all over town talking about me to anyone who would listen."

"No, Jack. I wasn't. I promise you that."

He nodded and glanced over my shoulder when a car pulled into the parking lot. "I'll be right back," he said. "Can you wait for a minute?"

"Sure."

After grabbing a clipboard, he headed outside,

giving me time to collect myself. I'd established I didn't harbor any ill will toward him, but I did worry about his girlfriend. She seemed mentally unstable and paranoid, and the conversation with Jack only reinforced the feeling for me.

Ten minutes later, he returned. "Well, they haven't heard I'm the town's big, bad killer. They just booked a Jeep tour for tomorrow."

"That's great," I said, truly happy for him. "Can we talk about Darla a little bit more?"

He sat down behind the desk. "Sure. What's up?"

"I think there's something wrong with her," I ventured. "She's acting... strange."

"Like how?"

"She's overly paranoid and thinks I'm out to get her."

Furrowing his brow, he shook his head. "Really? I haven't heard that, but I don't see much of her."

Wait. *What?* "You don't see much of her?"

"No. We grab a bite to eat every now and then, but that's about it."

Gosh. Perhaps I was the one losing touch with reality? But no, I recalled Darla had said she and Jack were dating. "She... um... she told me you two were an item."

Jack shot to his feet and planted his palms on the desktop. "What?!"

"Yes. She told me you were dating."

His mouth fell open and he stared at me as if waiting for the punchline. When none came, he asked, "What planet is that woman living on?"

"I don't know," I replied, now more worried about Darla than ever. She appeared to exist in an ulterior universe.

Jack ran his hand through his hair and sighed. "We aren't dating, Bernie. I've taken her out to lunch a few times, and we had dinner at the diner once... maybe twice. I thought we were friends."

"She obviously thinks you're more."

"I don't want a girlfriend."

"Jack, it's fine. There's something wrong with her and unfortunately, I think you're going to have to be the one to discuss it with her."

"Why me?"

"Because she trusts you. She cares for you, but she thinks I'm out to ruin her."

"What about her family?" He sat down again.

"They don't live here. They're in Idaho."

After muttering a few curses, he asked, "Who else can talk to her?"

"I don't know." I shrugged. "I barely see her and when I do, she's staring daggers at me."

Jack put his elbows on the table and placed his head in his hands. "It makes sense now, Bernie. All these little things she did... I understand it now."

"Like what?"

"Stupid stuff," he mumbled. "I'm so dumb."

"If she thinks I'm out to get her and that she's dating you, she has some problems, Jack. Right now, you are the one she's closest to, at least in her mind. You have to talk to her."

He nodded and leaned back in his chair. "You're right. I will."

"Thanks," I said, standing. "She doesn't want me around, but if there's anything I can do, let me know."

As I hurried to my car, I was left with more questions than when I'd arrived. What was going on with Darla? How would she react to Jack calling her out on her strange behavior?

What actions was he guilty of in his past? Was it something as diabolical as getting away with murder and figuring he could do it again in the case of Harold's death? Could Harold somehow be tied to Jack's questionable past? If Jack wanted to start over in Sedona, that meant cutting ties with those he left behind. He hadn't given any indication he'd known Harold, but what if he had? And did anything that had happened to him somehow drive him to murder?

This was a possibility and one that couldn't be overlooked. Jack had admitted he'd wanted to push Harold. Then, he'd hired a lawyer. Was Mr. Dimples a cold-blooded killer?

CHAPTER NINE

The next morning, Amy and Cathy checked out.

"I've decided to go with a venue in Phoenix," Amy said, sighing. "I talked to my mom and she doesn't think it's fair to make people drive up here."

"That's too bad," I replied, taking the key she handed me. "It's not *that* far."

"I know, but she's thinking about grandma and her sisters who don't like to drive anywhere outside a five-mile radius from their houses."

"Well, if you change your mind, we'll be here for you," I said. "Have a safe trip home!"

As soon as the front door closed behind them, I went to the cleaning closet, pulled out my buckets, and trotted up the stairs. Ruby materialized at the landing and I ended up walking right through her.

"Watch where you're going, Bernie!" she yelled.

"How about you watch where you appear?" I strode into the first bedroom. When I'd first been able to see Ruby, one of her favorite things to do was to scare me by revealing herself right in front of me. I'd yelp, she'd laugh. That had grown old pretty quickly, so now I usually walked right through her without a second thought, not giving her the satisfaction of showing a reaction.

"You're no fun anymore!"

I chuckled as I set down my cleaning supplies and pulled off the sheets. A moment later, Ruby joined me.

"What are we doing today?" she asked, perching on the edge of the dresser.

"I'm going to clean rooms, plant the petunias I bought yesterday, and then call Jack." Honestly, I thought he'd phone me the previous night, but I hadn't heard from him. Did that mean he hadn't had the opportunity to speak to Darla, or had he chickened out?

The petunias had been an impulse buy on my way home from Jack's. They'd caught my eye sitting in front of the nursery and I'd remembered Ruby used to plant them every spring in the big wooden barrels out front. I decided to follow in her footsteps.

"Ugh. We need some excitement around here, Bernie. Let's go see Adam and Old Coot Carl."

"That's not his name," I reminded her.

"We don't know that for sure."

"Well, based on the fact he called you Sea Hag Shirley when you did address him that way, I'm going to assume he doesn't like it when you call him that."

"His name *could* be Carl. Maybe he doesn't like the Old Coot part."

Who could blame him?

Ruby sighed. "Well, I don't recall him ever giving us his real name... only insults."

"After *you* insulted *him*." I turned to her. "*You* started it."

"Touché. Let's go see Adam and his roomie."

Adam and I had been playing phone tag for the past couple of days and I didn't want to show up on his doorstep unannounced. "He's busy helping the sheriff solve a murder," I said. "We'll see his ghost when he invites us over again."

"I'd love to know Old Coot Carl's story," Ruby mused. "How he died and stuff."

"We all would. However, he seems spooked by you."

"You're a crack-up," Ruby said, laughing. "A ghost who's spooked. Good one, Bernie."

I smiled as I made the bed, pleased with my unintentional humor. I'd been so preoccupied thinking about Darla, I hadn't given Adam's roommate much thought.

"So what did you think about Amy and Cathy?" Ruby asked.

"They seemed nice enough," I replied with a shrug. "It's too bad Amy won't be getting married up here, but I understand her mother's point of view. Highway 17 can get a bit tricky."

"That's true."

The door chimes rang downstairs and I pulled out my phone to check for notification of someone having made a reservation. Nothing. A walk-in, which I hated. Usually, it was someone who wanted to talk me down on my prices. I preferred when they paid online to secure the reservation and that way there wasn't anything to negotiate.

"Hello?" a man's deep voice called.

"I'll head down there," Ruby said, disappearing.

After running a hand over my hair and smoothing out my T-shirt, I shut the door to the room and hurried downstairs while bracing myself to remain firm on my pricing. A balding man with a midlife paunch carrying a small suitcase in one hand and a briefcase in the other stood in the living room.

"Hi," I said, smiling. "What can I do for you?"

"I was hoping you had a room available for me," he said, glancing all around the living room. "I was staying at one of the hotels, but I found it too noisy with all the tourists. I need somewhere quiet."

"Of course. I do actually have one available right now," I said. *Please just take it and don't haggle with me.*

"The death room," Ruby said, her voice deep and ominous. "Let's hope this guy doesn't bite it in there like Gonzalez did."

Yes, let's hope so. I strode over to the check-in desk and pulled out my iPad. After bringing up the reservation form, I handed the device over to him. "If you could please fill this out, we can get you that room."

"I wonder what his story is," Ruby mused as she strode up next to him. "Maybe a golfer? Probably not. He's too pasty. Doesn't get much sun. Based on that and the slacks and button-down shirt, he's some type of businessman who works too hard, I'd say. Probably a whisky drinker. Maybe tokes on a cigar every now and then as well."

"I... uh, I'm not good with technology," the man

said, handing me back the iPad. "I've got fingers like sausages. Can you type in my information?"

"Oh! Sure!" I replied. "Let's start with your name."

"Larry O'Malley."

"Ha! I was right! A nice Irish whiskey drinker," Ruby mused. "Ed McMahon once said, 'God invented whiskey to keep the Irish from ruling the world.'"

"Your address?" I kept my gaze focused on the screen instead of my grandmother spewing Irish insults.

"I need to get to Disneyland," I said when he announced he was from Los Angeles. "I love it there."

Ruby continued, this time in a horrible English accent. "Winston Churchill said, 'We have always found the Irish a bit odd. They refuse to be English.'"

Where was she getting this stuff? I'd never heard her quote anyone but the Rolling Stones, Lynyrd Skynyrd, and Janis Joplin.

"Phone number?" I asked.

"Let me give you my cell," he said.

Once the form was completed and I'd run his credit card, I grabbed the key to his room, or *the death room*, as Ruby liked to call it.

"I'm in town on business," Mr. O'Malley said. "I was wondering if it would be okay for me to conduct a meeting or two in the living room. It's such a comfortable space."

"Of course," I said. "That's fine."

"My meetings need to be private. Is that going to be an issue?"

I wasn't sure what he expected me to say. That I'd be happy to leave the house? I wouldn't repeat anything I heard?

He reached into his pocket and pulled out three-hundred-dollar bills and slid them across the desk. "This would be for your trouble."

I stared at the bills. Three hundred bucks would help me out a lot. Business had been brisk and I wasn't in bad shape financially, but the money could buy a lot of peanut butter and chocolate smoothies.

"You can put that toward a new ATV!" Ruby yelled. "Take the bribe! Grab the cash!"

She was right. Forget the smoothies. I'd been saving up for an ATV since I had to get rid of Ruby's, and the money would definitely move up the buy date.

However, I didn't want any trouble, and the situation reeked of it.

But, dang. The cash would be nice.

"Are you... are your meetings about illegal matters?" I asked. The last thing I needed or wanted was drug deals or something just as sinister taking place in my home.

"No. I assure you that everything is very legal. I'm a lawyer with a license to practice here in Arizona. Everything is very much on the up and up."

"I've known crooked lawyers," Ruby muttered. "In fact, they're all dirty in some way, shape or form. But that doesn't mean you shouldn't take the money. Grab it before he changes his mind, Bernie!"

"Your meetings aren't any of my business," I said, palming the cash and stuffing it into my jeans pocket. "I'm happy to tuck myself away in my private quarters or leave the house. Just give me some notice."

Mr. O'Malley sighed and nodded, then smiled. His relief was evident. "Great. Thank you for your understanding. I'll only be here a couple of nights, so I won't trouble you for very long."

"I'll show you to your room," I said. "Follow me."

After I led him up the stairs, I stopped at the death room. "This is yours. If there's anything you need, let me know."

He opened the door, glanced around the space then turned to me and nodded. "I will. This is perfect. Thank you." No sense in telling him a drug trafficker had met his demise in there.

I nodded as he shut the door, then returned to my cleaning across the hall.

I scrubbed down the bathroom and made the bed. Next came the vacuuming and dusting. Surprisingly, Ruby didn't join me. An hour passed and I moved on to the next room.

Once I finished cleaning, I examined both rooms with a critical eye, searching for anything I may have missed. The wooden furniture gleamed, the comforter and pillows sat neatly on the bed, the bathrooms showed no sign of a wayward hair, and the towels hung with precision from the racks. I didn't find anything else that needed to be done, but I'd check again tomorrow.

As I carried my supplies out into the hallway, I heard Mr. O'Malley's voice from the death room. The urge to listen in hit, but I kept walking and hurried downstairs.

Ruby followed me outside to the garage where I found my gloves and hand shovel. When we returned to the front of the house, she plopped down on the cement walkway and tilted her head up to the sun. "I can't feel it, but I bet it's a warm, beautiful day."

"It is," I said, wishing I had worn my hat. "A perfect day for sunscreen."

"The sun's good for you, Bernie."

"The sun gives you skin cancer and wrinkles," I retorted while plunging my shovel into the first barrel. "I don't know why you continue to argue with me about that. It's fact."

I glanced over my shoulder to find her watching me, a small grin on her ghostly face.

"It warms my cold, dead heart to see you keeping the barrels full of beautiful flowers," she said. "It's such a simple thing but brings so much happiness. Rule-eight-hundred-and-fifty-six of life: always plant the flowers."

"You're getting a little more sentimental the deader you become," I replied, smiling.

Ruby threw her head back and laughed. "Wouldn't that be something? Your old grandma becoming syrupy?"

"Yes, yes it would." I looked around the neighborhood. Surely at least half the town thought I was nuts because they'd seen me have conversations with an invisible person.

I planted four of the six barrels while Ruby remained seated on the concrete, humming softly. The lull of the neighborhood, the birds chirping in the distance, and Ruby's song relaxed me to the point that I almost screamed when my phone rang in my pocket.

Muttering a curse, I pulled off my gloves and dropped them to the ground. I answered without glancing at the screen. "Hello?"

"Hey, Bernie. It's Jack."

"Oh, my gosh." My shoulders sagged as I sank down to the concrete next to Ruby. "I've been waiting for you to call. Did you talk to her?"

"Yeah, I did."

"What happened?"

CHAPTER TEN

"Well, I went over to the diner and it was closed, but the door wasn't locked," Jack began. "So I went in, figuring she'd gone upstairs and forgotten to close up." Darla lived in a small apartment above the diner, a cute space that always smelled like roses and bacon. An odd combination, but somehow quite comforting. "She was lying on the couch, staring at the television. When I called her name, she barely glanced at me. For a second, I thought she was drunk or on drugs."

"Darla would never do drugs and the most I've seen her drink is a glass of wine on a Friday night," I replied. "She'd never—"

"I know, Bernie. I realized there was something

wrong with her. I ended up calling for an ambulance. She was completely out of it."

Tears pricked my eyes as I pursed my lips together. "What's wrong with her?"

"Before the ambulance came, I asked her if she wanted me to call someone. She shook her head, but just kept staring at the TV. I found her phone in the kitchen and used her finger to unlock it. She didn't fight me. It was like she didn't even realize what I was doing. When the EMTs took her to the hospital, I called her mother. She's coming out. But she told me that Darla suffers from schizophrenia. Did she ever tell you?"

My breath caught in my throat and I glanced over at Ruby who studied me carefully.

"What's he saying?" she whispered.

"No," I said. "She never shared that with me."

"Her mom said she's supposed to be on medication to help control it, and she asked me to search the apartment for the bottles. I found them, but they were full, and the date of the prescription was a month ago. It looked to me like she quit taking her meds."

"Why would she do that?"

"Good question. Her mother said she's done it before."

I thought I knew Darla, but apparently she'd been harboring a big secret. Why hadn't she shared this with me?

"Her mom asked me how she's been acting," Jack said. "I told her about her thinking you were out to get her and how she thought she and I were dating. Her mom said schizophrenia caused delusions and it only reaffirmed that Darla had gone off her meds."

"Oh, my word," I muttered, a wave of helplessness washing over me. The new information explained so much. Guilt settled in my chest as I recalled our last conversation. I hadn't exactly been nice. "What can we do to help?"

"Well, I'm not fully sure. After they'd taken her to the hospital and I finished up the phone call with her mom, I took a look around. The kitchen in the diner is a mess... rotting vegetables in the refrigerator and everything just looks dirty."

"Why aren't her employees picking up the slack?"

"Again, I don't have an answer, Bernie. The diner was closed when I got there. But even her house was messy."

"That's not like Darla," I muttered. The desire for neat and orderly surroundings was one thing we both shared.

"Her mom's flying in from Idaho tomorrow. I gave her your phone number and mine. For now, I don't know what else to do."

My mind spun with ways to help Darla and the best thing would be to start simple. Clean up her place. I had no idea what to do with the restaurant, though. I was happy to go in and scrub it down, but I lacked knowledge on how to run one. "What about the diner?" I asked. "If there's bad food and the kitchen's dirty, it could be a lawsuit waiting to happen if someone becomes sick. Or, if the inspectors come in, they could close her down."

"Agreed. I'm going over to talk to a couple employees right now, but in the end, I think the decision is up to Darla's mom."

"This is just... unbelievable, Jack. I had no idea."

"No one did, Bernie," he said with a heavy sigh. "I'll talk to you later, okay?"

"Sounds good." I set my phone down on the pavement and stared at it a moment.

"For the love of everything holy, what the heck happened?!" Ruby yelled. "Don't keep me in suspense!"

After I recapped the phone call, Ruby shook her head. "Crazier than a four-dollar bill."

"No," I snapped. "She has a mental illness that

isn't any different from a physical illness. It's just in her brain instead of her body. Would you be saying such things if I announced she had cancer? Or a heart problem? I hope not. Don't talk about her that way again."

I stood and clenched my fists in anger at both Ruby and myself. Rather than sulk in my own bitterness and despair, I should have realized something was wrong with my friend much earlier.

"Okay, okay," Ruby said, getting to her feet. "Message received and understood. Sheesh." She turned and glanced down at the street. "And by the way, you've got company."

I looked over my shoulder to see Adam pulling up in a sheriff cruiser. I grinned as my anger faded and my heart pattered. What a wonderful surprise.

He exited the vehicle and waved, but his usual smile was gone.

"He's either got bad news, or he's going to arrest you, or that is one depressed man," Ruby muttered.

"Hi," I greeted him as he approached, noting Ruby had been correct. With his sagging shoulders and tired gaze, he seemed defeated. "What's up?"

"Not a lot," he muttered. "I need to be cheered up so I thought I'd come see you."

I'd just found out my friend had a mental illness,

so I wasn't quite sure I was capable of giving him what he needed, but I'd give it a shot. "Sure. Come on in."

He followed me inside and I remembered I had a guest upstairs. Mr. O'Malley may have wanted privacy, but so did I. "Let's go into my bedroom," I said. Our voices wouldn't carry throughout the house from there.

As Adam sat on the bed, I closed the door and sank into my rocking chair. "What's going on?" I asked.

"We're at a standstill on Harold's murder," he said, rubbing his eyes. "I seriously have no idea what to do next. To make matters worse, the sheriff has put me in charge."

"Isn't that kind of a conflict since you were a witness?" I asked.

"Yeah, it is, but our caseload is so high, he says he doesn't have a choice. We've got a robbery at the grocery store, some kids spray painting stop signs, and the governor just announced some new police policies that we have to follow. Training manuals need to be written and classes need to be designed to make sure we comply with the order. The sheriff wants me to figure out who killed Harold, and either he or another deputy will make the arrest."

"So, I take it you've interviewed everyone?"

Adam nodded. "I've been over the reports a dozen times and nothing sticks out to me. Belinda and Nancy have some fancy-pants lawyer from California representing them, and he's not allowing them to say much."

"I'm sorry to hear that," I said.

"You know, we've got an attorney from California upstairs," Ruby said, a slow smile crossing her face.

Oh, my gosh. She was right.

"What are the chances of two fancy-pants lawyers from California being in Sedona after a murder?" Ruby mused. "And he did say that his meetings were private. What could require more privacy than meeting with your client about *murder*?"

"What's wrong, Bernie?" Adam asked. "You look pale. Are you feeling okay?"

I held up a finger as I stared at Ruby. Yes, what were the chances? How huge of a coincidence would that be? My guess hovered right at zero.

"I... I just thought I heard someone come into the house," I lied, completely unprepared to reveal the lawyer he spoke of was in my home at that exact moment.

"Should we go check?" Adam asked, glancing at the bedroom door.

"No, it's fine," I replied. "So how are you going to crack the case?"

Adam smiled and stared at me sheepishly. "Well, I've been through all the reports. I've watched the interviews, and like I said, I'm at a loss."

I nodded, my mind still focused on the fact I most likely had Belinda and Nancy's lawyer staying with me. Mr. O'Malley obviously hadn't recognized my name. There had to be some sort of legal problem with him representing two suspects and staying with a witness. Right? I didn't have a law degree, but it seemed like a definite conflict of interest.

"I really don't know what to do at this point, Bernie. I guess I'll start at square one. Interview everyone again, go over the reports for the millionth time. Someone has to slip up at some point and reveal the killer."

"Poor copper," Ruby said. "Sounds like he could use some help."

I agreed, but I had no idea how to assist Adam. I ran a bed and breakfast, not an intelligence agency.

"And to make matters worse?" Adam continued. "Frank, the sheriff's second in command, is retiring. Sheriff Walker is going to be filling that spot and he's mentioned that I may be up for the promotion. If I can solve this case, I have a better chance."

"Old Bruce Walker should be the one retiring," Ruby said. "What's he... ten years older than Frank? That man should be put out to pasture."

"I wish I could be a fly on the wall of the suspects' rooms," Adam said. "They're all staying at the Sedona Grand Hotel. One of them is a murderer. They have to be talking about it. They have to make a phone call or *something* and give themselves away."

"I'm sorry, Adam," I said. "I wish there was something I could do."

"I've got to get going," he said, standing. "It was so good to see you, Bernie. I miss you. Hopefully I'll catch whoever did this and we can spend more time together."

Our embrace lasted a long while, and Adam's desperation and disappointment of not being able to solve the murder was almost a tangible force.

I walked him to the front door and then headed back to my room. "I feel so bad for him," I said, sinking into my rocking chair once again.

"We can help him," Ruby said, a slow smile crossing her face. "I have an incredible plan."

Oh, no. That never meant anything good. "Help him how?"

"Well, he said he wished he was a fly on the wall of the suspects' room, but obviously, he can't turn into a fly. However, I can be in any room I want to be in without anyone knowing it. Well, except you, of course."

Staring at Ruby, I couldn't believe my ears. Was that legal? "You... you want to... spy?"

"Sure! This is right up my alley," Ruby said, rubbing her hands together. "It'll be more fun than the time I gave Cher a reading and we ended up having margaritas out by her pool. That woman's a hoot!"

While alive, Ruby had made her living as a psychic and done very well, even becoming a minor celebrity and having her own phone-in psychic line.

"What about my alley?" I asked. "In case you forgot, outside of this house you can't go more than fifteen feet away from me. I have to be close to you. What happens if I get caught while you're spying?"

Ruby shrugged. "Nothing happens. You just go on your way. No one knows you have a ghost with you who's listening in to help a cop at the end of his rope."

"I... I don't know if I'm comfortable with this," I said while Ruby twirled around in a circle. "Isn't that cheating somehow?"

"In a way, yes," Ruby said. "But the only ones who'll be aware of it are you and me."

"What about Adam? You said you wanted to help him. Wouldn't we have to tell him what you discover?"

"Hmm... I suppose so. Otherwise, it defeats the purpose, doesn't it?

"This is a stupid idea," I muttered, shaking my head.

"Don't be a downer, Bernie! We'll be like Starsky and Hutch. Frank and Ponch!"

"More like Scooby and Shaggy," I murmured as I shut my eyes and rubbed my temples.

I wanted to help Adam succeed. But I truly had a moral dilemma of whether I should use my ghost to gain access to information he shouldn't know about. "No matter what bits and pieces you may or may not overhear, Adam still needs to prove someone's guilty. No one can be convicted on the word of a ghost."

"You're right," Ruby said. "But at least we can give him an idea of where to concentrate his efforts. The more information he has, the better chance he'll have of solving the case."

"What do you think you're going to hear?" I asked. "Someone confessing?"

"If I'm lucky!"

"Oh, man, Ruby. I can't believe you."

"This is the most exciting thing that's happened around here since we found the body upstairs," she said. "Help out Adam. Help *me* out of this perpetual boredom you call your life. Let's do this."

"It may be illegal," I hissed. "I don't want to go to prison for anything."

Ruby threw her hands up in the air. "For what? What are you going to prison for?"

"For doing something illegal!"

"Existing is not illegal, Bernie. No one is going to realize that you have a ghost tagging along. If anyone should be worried about doing something wrong, it's me, and I'm certainly not concerned in the least bit."

"Why doesn't that surprise me?" I shook my head.

"Come on, Bernie. Just think... you could be dating the second in command at the sheriff's office. How sexy is that?"

I turned my stare to the window while considering my situation. First, I had the lawyer upstairs representing two of the murder suspects. Ruby could garner a lot of information from him. But not everyone involved was staying at my home. In fact, every other suspect except Jack was at the Sedona

Grand Hotel. Ruby was aware of that, and honestly, it was probably the best place to eavesdrop.

"What are we going to do, Bernie?" Ruby asked. "Are we going to play cops and robbers and help out that fella, or are we going to watch from the sidelines?"

I spent the next morning cleaning Darla's apartment and Jack made the call to shut down the diner when he noticed a roach scurrying across the floor. The employees were rightfully furious, but Jack felt he had to protect Darla and her livelihood, and frankly, I agreed. Until her mother arrived and made some hard decisions, we were going on instinct.

While mopping, vacuuming, and scrubbing, I tried to mind my own business. I truly did. But when I dropped a stack of books and found a diary, I had to take a peek. Tears came to my eyes as I tried to decipher the gibberish. I hoped she found the help she needed and got well soon.

In the afternoon, Ruby and I stood in front of the Sedona Grand Hotel, my palms sweaty, my chest aching with anxiety. How in the world had I allowed her to badger me into this plan?

With the hotel's white pillars and large windows. I had to admit, Ruby was right. I understood why it reminded her of a mausoleum.

"When I was alive, you wouldn't catch me dead in here," she muttered. "Bunch of pretentious jerks sitting around talking about golf and the stock market. Now that I'm dead, I'm actually walking through the doors." She let out a long sigh. "The things I do for you."

I rolled my eyes and shook my head. "Ruby, don't you dare try to make this about me. You're so excited to do this, you couldn't hide that smile if you tried."

"But it is about you," she said. "Adam's only going to fall more in love with you than he already is when he finds out you're a regular Columbo."

"That's ridiculous," I muttered. "Adam's not in love with me."

"Of course he is, dingbat," she said glancing down at her mumu. "I sure feel underdressed for our adventure, though. I need a trench coat and a fedora like *Columbo*."

I felt the same way, even though I'd worn the only blouse I owned instead of a T-shirt. But with my jeans and sneakers, I didn't fit in. Those entering the establishment wore tennis skirts, slacks, and dresses. I didn't belong, and I had no problem with that. I wanted to get in and out without an issue. "Just a little reminder—no one but me can see you. The trench coat and fedora wouldn't be noticed."

"Then give me a gun like in *Charlie's Angels*. I can already kick butt with my fists." Ruby with a gun would be a disaster of epic proportions and watching her punch the air and swing and kick her legs MMA style with her purple mumu flowing around definitely amused me. I stifled a giggle.

"How about if we just go inside before I change my mind?" I asked.

"Lead the way! I'm going to put James Bond to shame!"

As I strode in through the front door, Ruby trailed behind me humming the theme song to the *Streets of San Francisco*. The fact that I recognized it only indicated I needed to watch more television made in my lifetime instead of hers.

The large, white marble lobby gleamed as the sun shone in through the floor to ceiling windows leading out to a pristine blue pool. The golf course lay beyond that. A beautiful property, but definitely not Ruby's and my style. I'd never stepped foot in the hotel, either—never had a reason to.

"Dang, it's bright in here," she said. "Like that light at the end of my tunnel."

After Ruby died, she'd walked toward the light, but she'd never reached it. She did believe it was the gateway to heaven, but they wouldn't let her in.

"What room did Mr. O'Malley mention when he was on the phone?" I asked. While I cleaned Darla's place, Ruby had spent most of the morning in the lawyer's room listening in to his calls and reading his private papers over his shoulder.

"Three-twenty-two. Or wait a minute. Was it Two-thirty-three?"

I stopped in the middle of the lobby and scanned the area to make sure no one was paying us... well, me... any attention. "Please remember which one," I whispered.

"Okay, it's three-twenty-two."

"Are you sure?"

"Yes and no. But mostly yes."

I followed her to the elevator and we waited as people crowded around us. A woman moved into Ruby's space next to me.

"Watch it, sweet cheeks!" Ruby yelled.

The woman glanced at me, then stepped away as her nose crinkled. Ruby's distinct scent had that effect on some people.

We rode up the elevator to the third floor and found room three-twenty-two. When we stopped outside, I glanced to my right, then my left. No one could see Ruby, but I felt more exposed than a naked guy at church.

"I'm going in," she said, rubbing her hands together.

"Just a minute," I hissed, still scoping out the area. The doors to each room didn't sit flush to the wall, so there was a little space for me to hide. I wouldn't be visible to anyone unless they walked by.

With a deep breath, I whispered, "Okay, let's go."

Ruby raced a few steps ahead of me and ghosted through the door. I tiptoed up to it and tucked myself into the enclave. At first, I focused on the hallway to assure myself I wasn't about to be discovered, but soon I heard voices coming from the room—a man and woman. They spoke in low tones, so I couldn't make out what they said. I wondered who was with Belinda? Maybe Mr. O'Malley? After cleaning Darla's apartment, I'd stopped home to change before coming to the hotel, but I hadn't seen or heard him. A secret lover? Room service? I leaned my head against the panel to hear better, but my effort was futile.

A few moments later, Ruby came out.

"What happened?" I whispered as I followed her toward the elevator.

"Nothing," she replied, shrugging.

"What did they say? I couldn't make out anything. You weren't in there very long."

"They were discussing their son."

"Their son?" I furrowed my brow in confusion.

"Yes. Apparently, he's decided to quit college and start a band. Mom and Dad are pretty upset, but I don't see why. Let the kid have some freedom and work his creativity. For all they know, they have the next Paul McCartney waiting to blossom."

As we waited for the elevator, I tried to put the pieces together. Belinda was discussing her son... with whom? Did she have a child with someone other than Harold? Did they even have kids? It didn't make any sense. I glanced over at my ghost, the truth finally dawning on me. "You were in the wrong room, weren't you?"

"Darn right. It's two-thirty-three."

Figures.

Once we arrived on the second floor, the long brown hallway stretched silently in front of us. We found room two-thirty-three and I assumed my position as Ruby disappeared inside. Again, my attention was drawn to the voices behind the door, but this time, they were loud and clear. Well, Belinda was loud, but not very clear. In fact, she sounded drunk.

"I'm going to miss him," Belinda wailed. "Oh, Harold!"

"Of course you are," Nancy comforted. "He was your husband for many years."

"He was so awful, though." Belinda sniffled. "Such a jerk."

"Yes, he was."

"But he was *my* jerk. He was good to me. He loved me. I have to tinkle."

A loud bang sounded from just inside the door. "Who put that wall there?" Belinda muttered. The bathroom obviously sat off the entry and she was a little unsteady on her feet.

"Do you remember that time he shorted our gardener because he cut the hedges too small?" Belinda called.

"I do."

"And the time he told the kids' foster organization that he'd donate if the kids came and did some work around the house and earned the money?"

"Oh, yes. You were mortified."

"He was an awful human being," Belinda said, her voice fading. Perhaps she'd gone back into the main room?

"Belinda, I'm here for you," Nancy said. "You're going to make it through this."

"Did you know I've never pumped my own gas?" Belinda slurred. "He filled my gas tank for me every single week. I have no idea how much money I have. I don't know which bank it's at."

"We'll get it worked out," Nancy said patiently.

"I have no idea how to pay my taxes!" Belinda keened. "Or my bills! He took care of *everything* for me and now he's gone! What am I going to do?"

"I'll teach you how to do all those things," Nancy said. "Surely, Harold has everything organized in his office. We just need to find the paperwork and I can help you figure it all out."

"And they think I killed him!" Belinda shouted. "I didn't! I'd thought about it before, but I'd never follow through! Is there a wife around who hasn't thought about killing her husband? They can be so difficult sometimes, but I couldn't do it. Never!"

"Yes, husbands can be quite difficult. That's why I divorced mine."

"I just want to go home!"

"We'll be able to leave soon," Nancy soothed. "Shh, Belinda. You're upset, and rightfully so, but you have to try to relax."

"I'm dying of a broken heart."

"You aren't dying," Nancy said, sounding exasperated. "We'll get through this together."

Silence stretched for a long while, and I wondered where Ruby was. Glancing out into the hallway, I noted I was still in the clear—no one approached.

"I think I've had too much wine," Belinda said. "I'm so tired."

"Then go to sleep. I'm right here and I'll watch over you."

A few moments later, the television came on at the same time I heard voices down the hallway.

I couldn't be caught just standing in the enclave. As they approached, I stepped out into the hall and bent over to tie my shoe, hoping it didn't appear like I'd been hiding.

"Hello," I said, glancing up to find two hotel security guards coming toward me, one burly and muscular, the other thin and wiry. Both wore black pants and a white golf shirt with a nametag I couldn't read, either because of anxiety or I suddenly needed glasses. I swallowed back my fear and smiled.

"We have reports of someone yelling from this room," the burly guy said, pointing to Belinda's. "Are you staying in there?"

I shook my head. "Nope. Just tying my shoe."

"It seemed like you came from in there," the skinny one said, narrowing his gaze on me.

"Sorry, you're mistaken. I'm just leaving."

"What room are you in?" he asked, pulling out a phone. "Are you even staying with us?"

He most likely had the ability to look up a guest and find a corresponding room number with a few taps of his fingers. If I made up a room number, I'd be caught.

"I was visiting a friend," I replied, actually impressed with myself for lying so easily. "She's down that way, but I can't remember her room number."

They exchanged glances and nodded, which I took to mean I had been dismissed.

Ruby cursed our tether behind me as I hurried down the hall. "Slow down, Bernie!"

I shook my head and moved faster, wanting to put as much space between me and the security guards as possible before they called me back to question me further.

Instead of waiting for the elevator, I jogged down the stairwell. When I reached the lobby landing, I took a deep breath and smoothed down my blouse.

Ruby stood next to me and grinned. "That

woman was a cork high and a bottle deep. It looked like a lot of fun."

"She sounded absolutely wasted," I whispered as I pushed open the door to the lobby. After a quick look around, I beelined for the front entrance.

"Let's go check out the pool area," Ruby said. "Maybe this place isn't so bad after all."

I shook my head. "No."

"What are you afraid of?" Ruby said.

"Getting caught by security." Exactly what I had been worried about before entering the hotel.

"No one is coming after you. Relax, Bernie! You're calling attention to yourself racing out of here like you're farting jet fuel!"

I looked over my shoulder. Ruby, as usual, was correct. I was only making myself a target for speculation.

Slowing down, I fished out my keys and strode over to my SUV. Once inside, I laid my head back against the headrest and took a few deep breaths. If the security guards hadn't arrived, I would've been fine.

I turned to Ruby. "Belinda's pretty upset."

"Oh, yeah," she said, chuckling. "And pretty drunk. I'm glad she finally passed out because she could barely walk."

"I thought I heard her run into the wall."

"She'll probably have a bruise on her shoulder from that one. I'll tell you one thing, though... she's one heck of a lightweight."

"Why do you say that?"

"There was one bottle of wine and it wasn't even halfway empty. Unless she'd been drinking before we arrived and I didn't see the empties, she didn't even have two glasses."

"Huh. Maybe she doesn't drink often."

"So, where are we going now?" Ruby asked.

"Well, I was thinking we should go see Adam."

"Why would we do that?"

"Because I want him to know what we're up to."

"Really?"

I honestly didn't know. Transparency was important, but I didn't want him telling me that Ruby's idea was epically horrible. I already knew that, yet, I'd jumped in with both feet. Besides, any information I brought him would need an explanation of where it came from. I saw no choice but to let him in on our secret mission.

Time to change the conversation. "If you're nice, maybe you'll meet his ghost."

"Old Coot Carl's afraid of me."

"Please don't call him names."

"I'm not making any promises."

"Ruby..."

"I'll think about it, Bernie, but I'm still angry at him for pinging you with a book so I may have to have a few words with him."

Dang it.

CHAPTER TWELVE

———

"Hey!" Adam said as he opened the door. "Come in! I was just doing some work."

I glanced at the papers littering the couch and the coffee table, probably all having to do with Harold's murder.

After he cleared the sofa, he motioned for me to sit down. "Do you want some coffee?" he asked.

Being so late in the day, I probably shouldn't or I'd never get to sleep, but I also noted his computer open on the table in front of me. A quick scan of the screen revealed the transcript of Nancy's police interview. I just required a few moments alone to peruse it. "Sure. Coffee would be great."

"I'll brew a fresh pot. Lord knows I need some."

When I heard the water running in the kitchen, I grabbed the computer.

Q: How would you describe Belinda and Harold's marriage?

A: *The best way to explain is to say it... was one of convenience. He had his arm candy and Belinda's been very well taken care of.*

Q: Do you think they loved each other? Were there marital problems?

A: *I've been Belinda's friend for ages and she did confide in me quite a bit, but she didn't tell me everything. I can't fully answer that. Did she love Harold? Yes, on some level I believe she did. Were there marital problems? Yes. But isn't there in every marriage?*

Q: Did she ever mention she'd like to divorce Harold?

A: *Not that I recall.*

· · ·

Q: Tell me what happened that night.

A: *Well, we'd been on the tour for about an hour. Those two dreadful men came with us... Art and Trevor were their names, I believe. They were rude to Belinda when she asked them to quiet down because she couldn't hear the tour operator, Jack.*

Q: What did they say?

A: *They told her to shut up, to stick a sock in it. Then, Harold got involved. He could be a real jerk, and he let them both have it. Said that no lowlife loser talked to his wife that way. Made a few homophobic remarks—he thought they were gay—and questioned their status as humans and men. Everything was about status with that man. How much money did you make? How many cars were in your garage? And if he didn't deem you to have enough, he didn't believe he should grace you with his time and energy.*

Q: And then what happened?

A: *Harold and Trevor almost came to blows, threatening to beat each other up. I've never seen two grown men act so childishly. Jack told everyone to calm down, but it was too late for Harold. He pulled more of the same with Jack... that he'd never amount to anything and he was a loser.*

When we came to a stop on the cliff, everyone sort of went their own way. I needed space to clear my head. I've been around Harold most of my adult life and I still have a difficult time with his outbursts. I made sure to remove myself from the group and went for a little walk. The night was beautiful, and I'd never seen a moon quite as large or bright. It was stunning.

Q: When did you know Harold had gone missing?

A: Jack whistled for us to return to the Jeep. When we all arrived, Harold never joined us.

Q: Did you notice anyone lagging behind?

A: I believe Art was the last one to join us, but I'm not one hundred percent sure.

Q: And you don't think Art and Harold knew each other?

A: My guess is no. I don't think Harold knew either of those men. I certainly didn't.

· · ·

Q: If Belinda didn't kill her husband, who do you think did?

A: *Well, it wasn't me, so it had to be one of those men, or our driver, Jack. The way Harold spoke to him was horrible.*

"BERNIE, WHAT ARE YOU DOING?" Adam asked as he carried in two steaming mugs. "That's police business!"

Dang it. I'd been so wrapped up in my reading, I hadn't listened for Adam's approach. "I know," I replied, setting down the computer where I'd found it. "Curiosity got the best of me. I'm sorry."

"You can't be snooping in my work like that," he said softly.

"Tell him you already are," Ruby said. "Starsky and Hutch are here to save the day and solve the case!"

Pursing my lips, I debated whether I should. If he didn't like me reading from a computer, he'd most likely have a fit hearing that my ghost was spying on the suspects.

I turned to Adam and pointed at the computer.

"Do you actually think Jack killed him? Nancy sounds like she does."

"It can't be ruled out," he said, sighing. "I hate the idea of my friend going to prison, but he had words with Harold and he did get a lawyer, which makes him seem guilty."

I glanced back at the computer and pulled my hair over my shoulder to conceal my face. I didn't want him to see that I had knowledge of Jack's checkered past.

"You do that a lot," Adam said.

"Do what?"

"When you don't want me looking at you, you pull your hair around your face, like you're trying to hide."

"I don't know what you're talking about," I muttered as my cheeks heated. Was I really that transparent and obvious? Yes, yes, I was.

"Do you have information on Jack that I should be aware of?"

I briefly considered telling him everything Jack had shared, but then Ruby said, "Don't you be a snitch. Snitches get shanked."

Unsure of whether she spoke from experience or if she recalled it from years of television, I kept quiet. But she was right. Not my place to spill Jack's secrets.

"Bernie?" Adam said, pushing my hair behind my shoulder.

"You should talk to Jack about his lawyer. Not me."

Adam stared at me a moment then nodded. "I feel like there's a lot you aren't telling me, and not just about Jack."

I met his gaze and made a decision.

"So, where's your ghost?" Ruby interrupted. "I've looked everywhere... well, as far away from Bernie as I can get."

At least she hadn't been screaming for him.

Turning to her, relief swept through me. I could put off the conversation a little longer. "I haven't seen him,"

"I didn't know Ruby was here," Adam said.

"Yes. She's looking for your ghost."

"I have questions for him," Ruby replied. "I want to talk to him."

The ghost appeared behind her. After glancing at me as if looking for assurances he wouldn't be verbally assaulted again, he cleared his throat.

Ruby screamed and spun around. "You don't sneak up on people like that—whether they're dead or alive!"

To my surprise, he chuckled, apparently appreciating he got the upper hand on Ruby.

"What can I do for you?" he asked.

"Well, you and I got off on the wrong foot," Ruby said. "I thought I'd introduce myself. I'm Ruby."

He narrowed his gaze on her. "My name's Ned."

"It's nice to meet you, cowboy," Ruby said, grinning.

"I'm not sure if I can say the same."

With a snort, I reverted my stare back to Adam. Trust between the two ghosts would take time to build.

"What's going on?" Adam whispered.

"Ruby and Ned are talking."

"Ah, so he does have a name. Are they being decent to each other?"

I nodded and glanced back at them.

"You'll feel differently once we spend some time together," Ruby replied. "I'm a hoot to be around. *Fun* is my middle name!"

"From what I've seen, perhaps that should be *trouble*. Or *insanity*."

"How did you die?" Ruby asked, pointing at his bloodstained shirt.

"I was shot."

"I supposed this piece of advice is irrelevant now,

but it's always best to avoid the business end of a gun." Ruby looked over her shoulder and pointed at me. "Remember that, Bernie."

Duly noted.

Ruby crossed her arms over her chest. "Here's the deal, Ned. You're dead. I'm dead. Neither of us should be here. So instead of calling each other names and throwing books, let's figure out why. How does that sound?"

Ned arched his eyebrow, still unsure of this new facet of Ruby. "I'll think about it."

As he faded away, Ruby shook her head. "That man has some trust issues."

"Can you blame him?" I asked. "By the way, I'm very impressed with this new diplomatic side of you."

Ruby rolled her eyes and waved her hand in front of her face. "So, when's Adam going to arrest the wife?"

Right. Back to *that* conversation. I cleared my throat and smiled sweetly. "Adam, Ruby and I have done something you aren't going to like. I wasn't going to tell you about it, but if I don't, I'm lying to you, and that makes me feel really gross."

He stared at me a long moment, then nodded. "What is it?"

"Remember when you said you wanted to be a fly on the wall in the same room as the suspects?"

"Yes."

"Well, Ruby went into Belinda's hotel room," I began. "I waited right outside the door and heard most of what was said."

"You... you what?"

"We spied on Nancy and Belinda to get you information on your case."

Ruby sighed. "I never imagined I'd be helping a copper. Death must have made my brain wonky. I'm doing all sorts of things I'd never do while alive."

"That's... you could get in a lot of trouble for that, Bernie!"

"I know, I know, but what's done is done."

"Was this Ruby's idea?"

"Of course it was. She convinced me we needed to help you."

Adam stood and began pacing the room muttering something about the fourth amendment.

"You have a lot on the line with this case," I said. "I want you to succeed. Ruby and I can do this for you."

The room fell silent. I picked at my cuticles hoping Adam didn't hate me. I wanted him to know what I was doing not only because I didn't want to lie, but also because the truth became a layer of protection for me. Someone would know where I was and I could reach out for help if needed.

Still, I couldn't believe I let Ruby talk me into her plan. If I didn't care for Adam so much, I'd have told her to go pound sand.

"What did you hear?" he finally asked.

As I recounted the conversation, he stared at me so hard, I thought laser beams may stream out of his eyes.

"Well, at least we've learned the stories about her husband are true," Adam said when I'd finished. "He wasn't a nice man."

"Tell him she was drunk," Ruby cut in.

I turned to her. "Why?"

"It may be an important clue," she replied with a shrug.

"Ruby wants me to tell you Belinda was wasted. Like running into walls and slurring her words drunk."

"That's not exactly a crime."

"She wanted you to be aware of it." I shrugged.

"Based on what you heard, do you think Belinda could have done it, Bernie?"

"I don't know," I replied. "She and Harold were apparently very wealthy. She *said* she has no idea how much money they have, but with him out of the way, it's all hers."

"With him being such a jerk, she's got two motives: getting rid of him and inheriting money."

As I recalled the conversation, I realized I hadn't fully processed what I'd heard. I'd been too worried about getting caught. "Belinda had it pretty good... or pretty bad, depending on the way you look at it. She has no idea where all their money is, how to pay her bills. She's never even pumped her own gas. Harold took care of everything for her."

"That's amazing, especially in this time period."

"It is." I couldn't imagine a life like hers. Had she been pampered, or should it be labeled something far more sinister? "It's like she had the freedom that money offers, but she was still imprisoned by him."

I hadn't heard any mention of children, and if there were, I would think that caring for them would be foremost on her mind. If she didn't know where the money was and how to access it, how would she put food on the table? Or maybe any offspring they might have had were grown and no longer financially dependent on her? "Do they have children?"

Adam shook his head. "No. Nancy said Harold never wanted any, so they'd skipped kids."

"What about Belinda? Did she want any?"

"Nancy said yes. It was a bone of contention between the couple."

"So, Belinda and Nancy have been friends for a long time."

"Yes, they have. Nancy is an intricate part of Belinda's life. A true friend and confidant."

"Belinda sure seems distraught," I said. "Can someone fake something like that after killing someone?"

"Sure she can," Ruby said. "If I were married to that turd, I'd have pushed him and played up the part of the grieving widow. She's rich now and doesn't have to put up with him."

Turning to Adam, I said, "Ruby's convinced Belinda killed him."

He nodded. "I'm leaning that way as well. But I have to be able to rule out everyone else."

"Let us help you, Adam." I stood and circled my arms around his waist and laid my head against his shoulder hoping to convey a bevy of emotions: regret for sticking my nose where it didn't belong, and the desire to help him succeed. Not that I cared whether I dated the second in command at the sheriff's office, or a deputy, but I could see how badly Adam wanted the promotion and to solve the murder.

But then there was that whole gray area of legalities. Ghosts don't exist. So was it truly wrong for Ruby to eavesdrop?

"I'm angry at you for spying on Belinda and Nancy, but also touched that you would want to help me. It could be dangerous, Bernie."

"But I'll tell you where we are and what we're doing. You can swoop in and save the day."

"It's a waste of energy to look into anyone else," Ruby said. "Belinda did it, end of story. But then again, it's not like I've got anything better to do. Nothing but time on my hands, so I'm in, although I do wish I had the trench coat and fedora I spoke of earlier."

"What's next, Adam?" I asked. "Where should we go from here?"

He sighed heavily and shook his head. "I can't believe I'm going to say this, but I want you to look over the statements from Art and Trevor and give me your thoughts, but I have to get to the office. In the meantime, are you free tomorrow morning?"

CHAPTER THIRTEEN

Golf. I'd gone once in my life and regretted the time wasted ever since. I simply don't have the patience to chase a ball over acres and acres of grass and swing at it with a club.

"I love golf," Ruby said from the seat next to me. On her insistence, Adam had rented a cart so we didn't have to walk the full eighteen holes. I wouldn't have minded the exercise, but when she pointed out how much sun we'd be getting, I acquiesced. "I used to go golfing with Sheriff Walker," she continued. "It's so quiet out on the course, and then my favorite part is the beer lady driving around."

"Golf is a boring game," I muttered.

"You obviously didn't drink enough beer when you played," Ruby said with a shrug.

Touché. I hadn't had a drop.

The grass seemed to stretch for miles. To the left stood a forest of pine trees, and to the right were amazing views of the red rocks. I had to admit, it was a very pretty place to spend the day.

Adam hurried out of the clubhouse and slid in the driver's seat. "Ready?"

"Yes," I replied. "But there's one more thing I think you should know."

"What's that?"

"I have a lawyer from California staying with me who says he has a license to practice in Arizona. He said he was at a hotel but he needed a quiet place to meet his clients. As Ruby pointed out, there is a pretty low chance that there are two lawyers from California here who are working right after a murder has taken place. I think it may be Belinda's guy."

"Holy cow," Adam whispered. "What's his name?"

"O'Malley."

Adam sighed and shook his head. "Unbelievable. That's him. Why didn't you tell me about this yesterday?"

"Honestly, I forgot about it. I was too worried about revealing what Ruby and I had been up to at the hotel."

"Fair enough," Adam said. "I'm assuming Ruby's been visiting him as well?"

"Yes," I said. "But she hasn't reported much of anything except Belinda and Nancy's room number."

"Not much going on in there," Ruby said. "Besides, I don't speak legalese very well."

With her record, I would think she'd be well-versed, but then again, she'd never been accused of murder.

"Let's get moving," Adam said, starting the cart."

"Woohoo!" Ruby yelled.

I sighed as I pulled on my baseball hat.

"Now remember, Art and Trevor had a tee-off time fifteen minutes ago," Adam said. "We should be able to catch up to them without a problem."

"Got it," I replied. "We're supposed to be surprised when we run into them."

"Exactly," Adam said, snickering. "And the fun tidbit of today: according to Ruby's jacket, she was arrested at this golf course for streaking a few years before she died."

"Aww... he remembers my record!" Ruby gushed. "That's so darn sweet."

"Why in the world would you strip down on a golf course?" I asked.

"Why not? The urge overcame me."

"I'm guessing that beer woman you mentioned had visited you a few times," I said.

"Well, yes, she had. You're very perceptive, Bernie."

"Okay, let's get out of here," Adam said, pulling onto the trail.

"Can you tell him to drive faster?" Ruby asked. "What is he? A hundred and two?"

When we reached the first hole, Adam exited the cart and went to the back to pull out a club. As he lined up his shot on the tee, Ruby also got out and began to dance. "What a beautiful day!" she yelled as she bounced around Adam. "Bet you can't hit me, copper! Give it your best shot!"

Clueless to the chaos that had descended on him, Adam stared straight ahead, managing his grip on the club.

"Come on, copper! What are you waiting for? Christmas? A written invitation? Hey, batter, batter, batter... swing!"

He gazed at the ball at his feet and slowly raised the club behind him. For a second, he froze, then brought his club down and turned to me. "She's right here, isn't she?" he called. "Is she taunting me? I swear I feel like someone is taunting me."

I nodded and burst out laughing as Ruby continued her antics.

"Ruby, I can't concentrate!" he said, laughing. "Knock it off, woman!"

Thrilled that she was being addressed, Ruby only became louder and after a minute, lay down right on the tee in fits of giggles.

Adam finally got his shot off, and they walked back to the cart, side by side.

"What was she doing?" he asked, sliding in.

I shook my head and smiled. "You don't want to know."

"I can't see her, I can't hear her, but I swear I'm beginning to sense when she's around."

"Ha!" Ruby shouted. "I'm going to be testing you on that one, copper!"

We drove up ahead to the second hole. More antics ensued. Adam told Ruby to leave him alone, but of course, this only drove her to become more annoying. Was he really beginning to sense when she was near him, or was he just saying that?

He shot the ball, and by the third hole, we'd caught up with Trevor and Art. The silly mood quickly became more serious.

"Okay, here we go," Adam said. "The tall, bald guy is Trevor. The other one is Art. Remember, we're just two people enjoying a golf game and we've run into them."

"Right. Is there one we should be paying more attention to than the other?"

"Well, Nancy said Art was the last one to join the group on the cliff after Harold had been pushed, so let's keep an eye on him."

I nodded, suddenly nervous. It was one thing to spy on people, but to confront them face to face gave me sweaty palms.

"Let's grab you a club and mosey on over."

I exited the cart with him and he handed me one. Together, we strode up to the tee.

"What a surprise to find you two here!" Adam said, once we'd arrived. The men turned at his voice. As their faces fell, I knew they weren't happy to have the police interfere with their day on the course.

"What can we do for you, Deputy?" Art asked.

"Nothing! Nothing at all," Adam said. "We're just out enjoying this beautiful day."

Art turned back to the course and lined up his shot.

"Nicely done," Adam said after he'd swung. "Looks like you're going to be right on target."

Next up was Trevor. He cursed after his ball veered into the trees.

"Listen, I just realized that I do have a couple of questions for you guys," Adam said. "Can we talk for a few minutes?"

The two men exchanged glances.

"Or I could have you come down to the station," Adam continued. "Personally, I'd much rather stay out here and I promise not to take too much of your time. It's a gorgeous day, isn't it?"

"What do you want?" Trevor said.

"Just a couple follow-up questions."

"Go ahead."

"You two didn't know Belinda, Harold, and Nancy. Correct?"

"We've already answered this," Art grumbled. "We live in Seattle. They're from Los Angeles, if I remember correctly. How in the heck would we know them?"

Adam nodded but I wasn't buying the answer. The world figuratively grew smaller every day, the internet playing an important role. People virtually gathered from all over the globe. It was quite possible that someone from Seattle knew another from Los Angeles.

Still, there was no way to prove them wrong.

"Trevor, you and Harold almost came to blows. Is that right?"

The tall, bald man nodded. "That guy was a sorry excuse for a human being. Yes, I wanted to rearrange his jaw, but I didn't kill him."

"And where were you two when Harold was killed?"

"Both of us had wandered as far away from that crew as we could," Art said. "We'd paid good money for the tour, and we wanted to enjoy it. I'd noticed that Harold and Belinda had walked toward one side of the cliff, so Trevor and I went the opposite way. The moon that night was spectacular."

"So you two were together the whole time up there?"

Trevor and Art exchanged glances and nodded.

I recalled in Nancy's statement to the police that she mentioned Art being the last one to join the group when Jack whistled for everyone to return to the Jeep. Either she'd been mistaken, or lied, or these two were having trouble recalling the truth.

"If you had to make a guess, who would you say killed Harold?" Adam asked.

I found the question interesting because he was acting as if he'd cleared the men from suspicion, but he obviously hadn't or we wouldn't be out on the golf course orchestrating a run-in.

"I have no idea," Trevor said. "Belinda seemed

like she was drunk, so I'm not sure if she even had the strength to push her husband. But if I had to guess, I'd say it was her."

"Same here," Art said, nodding his head. "That woman has some problems, though."

"When can we head home?" Trevor asked. "We'd like to return to Seattle as soon as possible."

"I really appreciate you guys hanging out," Adam said. "We're close to making an arrest, so maybe two to three days, if not sooner."

"You're going to make an arrest?" Art asked, pushing his mirrored sunglasses up his nose.

"Yes," Adam replied. "We're just tying up some loose ends, but an arrest is imminent."

"That's great news," Trevor piped up, smiling.

"I'll see you two later," Adam said. "Enjoy your game!"

As we strode back to the cart, I glanced over my shoulder to find the two men talking to each other. What were they saying?

"Go back to the cart," I said to Adam, handing him my club. "Ruby and I are going to listen in."

"Wait!" Adam hissed. "Bernie, don't!"

After making sure they weren't looking in my direction, I dashed over to the forest area, Ruby trailing behind me. Crouching behind a tree, I noted

Trevor had one hand fisted at his side while their faces were inches apart. Things seemed to be getting a little heated. Spying a tree with a thick trunk, I ran up to it and braced my back against it. "See if you can get close enough to hear anything," I whispered to Ruby.

"Aye, aye, Captain," she said, saluting me.

I peeked around the trunk to find her a few feet away from the arguing men. They may have been upset, but they spoke in low, harsh tones. She tried to move forward, but our tether held her in place. With no other trees to hide behind, I was as close as I could get.

Adam drove by slowly and stopped in an area where he and the cart would be hidden from Art and Trevor. I pressed myself against the trunk as though I may become one with it, the bark digging into my back. My breath came in short spurts and my heart thundered while I tried to think of excuses I'd give for hiding in the trees if the two men caught me. The only thing that came to mind was the need to pee. At least I was in Adam's sightline, so I relaxed a little. If I was discovered, Adam could come to my rescue if need be.

Not daring to look around the tree again, I waited for Ruby to return and strained to overhear the conversation. Unfortunately, a noisy crow also decided to let his presence be known in the branches above me. Any hopes I had of picking up bits and pieces were quickly swept away with the breeze.

The moments stretched on and finally Ruby showed herself at my side.

"What happened?" I whispered.

"Stay here just a little while longer," she said. "They're walking the course, so they don't have a cart. They just left, but they'd still be able to see you."

She stood next to me whistling while rocking from her toes to her heels, her hands laced behind her back. I remained still as I waited for her to give me the all-clear.

"Okay, we're good to move," she finally said, heading toward Adam in the awaiting cart. I let out a breath I didn't realize I'd been holding and followed. Relief washed through me when I glanced over my shoulder and didn't find any sign of Art or Trevor.

"What happened?" Adam asked as I slid into the seat next to him, Ruby following me.

"Yes, what happened?" I asked, turning to my ghost.

"Not a lot," Ruby said. "It was hard to hear them. I wanted to move closer, but I couldn't."

"Did you understand anything they said?" I asked.

Ruby shrugged. "I thought I heard them say that 'they have to let her know.'"

"Let who know what?"

"I have no idea. If it relates to the murder, the only two chicks involved are Belinda and Nancy," Ruby said. "And they all claim they've never met. But then again, it may be one of them has to call his wife and tell her he's on his way home in a few days."

"What's she saying?" Adam asked as he drove.

After I relayed the information, he banged his hand on the steering wheel. "I was hoping we'd get something more out of this trip."

"Like what?" I asked.

"Beats me," Adam muttered. "You scared me to death darting into the forest like that, Bernie."

"I'm sorry," I said, guilt settling heavily in my chest. "I saw an opportunity for Ruby to listen in on them and I took it."

"I'm not upset with you. It's everything about this case. I appreciate you and Ruby more than you'll ever know. I just wish you would've given me notice on what you intended to do."

Feeling a little bit better about everything, I

squeezed his hand. "It was a spur of the moment idea."

Adam chuckled. "I could see that."

Of course, Adam was correct. What I had done could have been very dangerous.

"Are we heading back now?" I hoped the day of golf would be blessedly cut short.

"No!" Ruby wailed. "Dang it! We're just getting started!"

I didn't relay her sentiments of opposition.

"Yeah, I guess we better," Adam said, sighing. "I've got to figure out who they're discussing and what information needs to be passed on. This dang case makes no sense to me."

CHAPTER FOURTEEN

Ruby and I headed home and she complained the whole way. Once we were inside, she disappeared—probably to her tunnel, which was fine with me. I needed a little time alone before Adam swung by after he made a stop at the office. He said he'd shouldn't be more than an hour.

The low tone of Mr. O'Malley's voice filtered down the staircase. I debated whether to head upstairs and listen in. Now I was waist-deep in this case and determined to find out who had killed Harold, not only to help Adam, but because he was right: the case made no sense, and I had the distinct feeling more than one person was lying. Not that I expected a murderer to be an honest, law-abiding citizen, but I hated liars—a trait Ruby and I both shared.

I climbed the stairs, avoiding the spots where they creaked. When I reached his room, I carefully pressed my head against the panel.

"How's Daddy's little girl?" O'Malley said. "I miss you."

I retreated quickly. I wouldn't be garnering any important information listening to him talk to his child. Although, he'd definitely had the kid later in life, or he was much younger than he appeared. With his bald head and extra tire around the middle, I pegged him to be in his late fifties or early sixties.

As I threw my baseball cap onto the rocking chair and fell onto the bed with a long sigh, my phone vibrated in my pocket. With a groan I pulled it out and read the notification I had a reservation in two days. At least I didn't have to do a deep clean on any of the rooms—just a quick spot check.

As my mind wandered while I waited for Adam, I couldn't help but think of Darla. I hoped she was okay and her mother would call me with an update when she had the chance.

I must have drifted off because the next thing I knew, a tapping at the back door in the kitchen woke me and I found Elvira sitting on my chest, purring loudly. "I didn't feel you climb aboard," I said, stroking her back. "But I have to go answer that."

Setting her aside, I rose from the bed and strode out into the kitchen. Adam smiled as I opened the door.

"Is O'Malley here?" he whispered, shifting his backpack from one hand to the other.

"I think so," I replied. "He was when I got home, but I just woke up so I'm not sure if he left or not."

"I thought I'd come in the back way to avoid seeing him," he said.

Smart idea. He wouldn't like the officer investigating his clients' murder hanging around. "Let's go into my bedroom," I replied.

Adam sat on the bed and I took the rocking chair. After unzipping his backpack, he pulled out his laptop and fired it up. A moment later, he handed it over to me. "This is the transcript of the police interview with Trevor. You can skip to the second page. The first is just his name, age, address and all that garbage. I highlighted what I want you to read."

I scrolled down to the second page and read the yellow area.

Q: What can you tell me about that night?

A: *I can tell you Harold was a jerk and I'm not sad he's gone.*

Q: That seems to be a recurring sentiment. Tell me about when you arrived up at the cliffs.

A: *I couldn't wait to get out of the Jeep. It was like a pressure cooker in there.*

Q: It's my understanding that you and Harold almost came to blows.

A: *That's true. He did threaten to fight me.*

Q: Where did you go once you were on top of the cliff?

A: *Art and I walked over to the opposite edge of where Harold and his wife had gone. I couldn't wait for the tour to be over and we talked about maybe asking for our money back.*

Q: That bad, huh?

A: *Yeah. But it wasn't Jack's fault, so we decided against asking for the refund.*

. . .

Q: When was the next time you saw Belinda?
A: *When Jack whistled for us all to return.*

Q: Did she seem okay at that point?
A: *Yes. A little off-balance, but yes.*

Q: In regard to who came back to the Jeep in what order, where did she fall?
A: *She was the last one.*

WAIT. Was that right?

I glanced up at Adam. "Didn't I read Nancy thought Trevor was the last one back to the Jeep?"

"I'll have to double-check to be certain, but yes, it rings a bell."

Returning my gaze to the screen, I continued reading.

Q: And you didn't know anyone from the group, correct?

A: *That's right... except Art. We came here to golf and get out of the Seattle rain. What a mistake that was.*

"NOTHING IS ADDING UP," I said. "Everyone is contradicting everyone else."

"Yup. I want to tear my hair out over this."

"Have you talked to Trevor and Art more than once? Besides on the golf course?"

"Yes. And they stick to their stories, which don't match up."

"What do you mean?" I asked.

"Give me the computer and I'll pull up Art's interview."

I handed the device over to him, once again wondering how many rules and laws we were breaking by him letting me read official police reports.

"Here," he said, handing it back to me. "Read the highlighted area."

Q: You didn't know anyone besides Trevor, is that correct?

A: *Yes. Thank goodness. Horrible people.*

. . .

Q: And who was the last one back at the Jeep when Jack whistled for all of you to return?

A: *Hmm... I don't recall. I think it may have been Nancy. Or Trevor. I'm not certain.*

"EITHER EVERYONE IS REMEMBERING things differently, or no one is telling the truth," I muttered, shaking my head.

"They've done studies on this," Adam said. "A group of people can experience the same event, but everyone's perception of what happened will be different."

"Do you think it's the case here, or do you think they're lying?"

"I don't know. No one knew a murder had occurred until we got there. Everyone acted as if he'd jumped. But we saw the fight and watched him go over the edge. *Someone* knew what had happened. So someone is lying."

He pulled out a pad of paper and drew a line. "This is the road leading up to the cliff," he continued, then sketched a large area which resembled a figure eight. "This is the top of the cliff, and right here is where Harold went down." The X was in the upper left side of the top of the eight.

I recalled the trail leading to the area when we'd searched for where he fell.

"According to Nancy, she was down here," Adam said, drawing a *N* at the bottom left side of the eight. "Art and Trevor were over here." *AT* was written at the top right of eight. "If Belinda pushed him then went back to the Jeep, that means Trevor was telling the truth. But if Nancy was being honest, Trevor was the last one to return to the group, which means he'd have to cross over this way and then push him."

"Without Belinda being there," I said.

"Exactly. And I don't know if you recall, but that's some rough terrain to cross right in that area to get from one side of the cliff to the other."

"It makes the most sense that Belinda's the killer. She's got motive and she had opportunity. I feel like she's being treated with kid gloves," I said. "I understand she may be the grieving widow, but as Ruby said, she could be faking it to make sure she doesn't get caught."

"I thought the sheriff went pretty easy on her," Adam agreed. "Based on what everyone has said, she's got an alcohol problem. Honestly, I could see her tripping, running into her husband, and having him fall off the ledge."

"But that's not what we saw," I said. "We witnessed two people fighting."

"True. But does she have the physical strength to fight her husband while she's drunk and push him?"

"I don't know. Also, did she have the pent-up rage that would have driven her to do it?"

Adam sighed and ran his hand through his hair. "What if... what if this is something else?"

"What do you mean?"

"What if it's not as cut and dry as a scorned wife offing her horrible husband? Or some guy being so angry, he decides to kill a stranger?"

"Like what?" I asked, thoroughly confused.

"I have no idea. I feel like there's something I'm not seeing."

I sighed and handed the computer back to him. "None of them knew each other. Of that we're certain because Jack confirmed it."

"He's still a suspect," Adam reminded me. "I can't take him off my list."

"Okay, so then you have the wife who's fed up with her husband's behavior, and three strangers who are angry enough to send him off a cliff."

"Three?"

"Jack, Art, and Trevor."

"What about Nancy?"

"Sure, she could have done it as well, but why? What's her motive?"

Adam shrugged. "Maybe she was having an affair with Harold and he told her he wasn't leaving his wife?"

That hadn't occurred to me. Some investigator I was.

"Who does Jack say was the last person to return to the Jeep?" I asked. "Who was the first one?"

Adam focused on the laptop as his fingers moved over the keyboard. "He says he can't remember who was the first one back. He wasn't paying attention. The report says he thinks Nancy may have been the last one, but he wasn't sure."

"I don't know what to think," I muttered, my frustration now mirroring Adam's. "But you're right —we're missing something. For all we know, it could have been someone up there that we aren't even aware of."

"But none of the tour group recall seeing anyone else on that cliff. And Jack's Jeep was the only vehicle."

"Someone could have hiked up there."

"And just decided to push Harold?"

"Maybe," I said, shrugging. "Maybe there's a psychopath loose in Sedona."

Just then, Ruby appeared wearing a Cheshire grin. "I know something you don't know," she said in singsong.

"You sound like a child," I muttered, really in no mood for her antics.

"You should be interested in the information I have," she said, sitting right next to Adam. "And if you're not, the copper here will be."

"Ruby's right next to me, isn't she?" Adam said. "My arm just got cold."

I nodded and sighed. "What's your big secret, Ruby?"

"Not going to tell until I know my payment," she said, the sly smile still in place.

"Your payment?" I asked. "What the heck does that mean?"

"Well, I wanted to stay and golf, but you wanted to come home. My fun was ruined, so therefore, you owe me."

"Ruby, you're dead," I said through gritted teeth. "You can't play golf."

Her smile faded and she tilted her chin up as she glared at me. "I'm very aware of that, Bernadette. It doesn't mean that I can't enjoy the day out on the course."

I winced. She never called me by my full name, so I knew I'd made her very upset.

"What's going on?" Adam asked.

"Ruby has information to share, but she wants payment for it because we left the golf course and ruined her day."

"What does she want?" Adam asked, glancing to his side.

"Yes, tell us," I said, hating that I was caving to her childish demands. "What do you want?"

"I'd like to go golfing again."

I rolled my eyes. "Forget it."

Ruby pointed a finger at me. "You better rethink your stance, young lady. The information I have could crack this case wide open."

I considered my options. Where could she have gotten her new knowledge? My guess was she'd been visiting O'Malley upstairs. And if he'd been on phone calls, she could have very well heard something incredibly important.

Or she could be playing me, having me make promises to her for nothing.

"What does she want?" Adam asked.

"To go golfing again."

Adam grinned and glanced over at the empty

space beside him. Well, empty to him. My ghost smiled at him sweetly. "I'd be happy to go golfing with the two of you," he said. "I wish we could've stayed out as well."

Ruby stood up and clapped her hands while dancing a little jig. "What a nice copper he is!"

I softened a little to the idea. Golf still would be considered one of my least favorite pastimes, but if Adam was there, maybe it wouldn't be so bad. Beautiful course, nice weather, and a visit or two from the beer lady wouldn't hurt either.

"Fine. We'll go. Now tell me this incredibly important information you have," I said.

Ruby sat back down, crossed her legs, and smoothed her hand over her purple mumu. "In a half-hour, Nancy will be meeting with Mr. O'Malley here at the house. And since you've promised me we're going golfing, I plan to listen in."

I gasped and brought my hand to my mouth.

"What?" Adam whispered. "What did she say?"

After I explained what would happen, Adam shot to his feet and packed up his laptop. "I can't be here. You're going to have to report back to me."

"We will," I said, opening the bedroom door. I walked out into the kitchen to be certain O'Malley wasn't in sight. When I heard him upstairs, I waved for Adam to come out of the bedroom.

Just as I shut the back door, I heard the staircase groan. A few moments later, O'Malley rounded the corner into the kitchen where I was pouring a glass of wine and trying to appear calm and nonchalant. With my knowledge of the upcoming meeting, the room had become quite warm.

"I'm going to need that privacy that we spoke of," O'Malley said after we engaged in a little small talk.

"Of course," I said. "I'll be in my room watching television. The living room is yours."

He thanked me and returned upstairs. As soon as the door shut, Ruby materialized next to me. "Your secret spy is reporting for duty."

"I think I'm going to be sick," I whispered. "This can't be legal."

"Nothing really fun ever is, kiddo," she said, rubbing her hands together. "Now quit your worrying and let's get a plan in place."

CHAPTER FIFTEEN

I stood in my bedroom with my head against the door. I'd lied to O'Malley. I'd rarely watched television until I'd discovered my grandmother, and I certainly didn't have one in my bedroom.

As I listened intently, I worried Ruby wouldn't be able to catch the full conversation. Of course, she could sit right there on the couches with the lawyer and Nancy, but she also had the concentration level of a gnat. More than once I'd been talking to her and she'd zoned out, not remembering anything I'd said the past few moments when I called her on her faraway gaze. She became bored so easily.

Adam would have to let all the murder suspects head home soon, or he'd put them in jail. With the big shot O'Malley in the picture, Nancy and

Belinda would be gone before they'd even settled into their cell. The miles between Los Angeles and Sedona would only make Adam's job more difficult. I wanted to help, and I didn't think I could fully rely on Ruby to report back on the conversation.

So, I was going to record it.

With a sweaty hand, I opened the door and glanced out into the kitchen. Nancy and her lawyer's voices carried my way from the living room. I grabbed my phone from the dresser, then dropped to my knees and slowly crawled out to the kitchen and hid behind the counter that separated me from the dining and living rooms. I leaned back against the cabinets and prayed no one would suddenly need a glass of water. If so, I'd be busted. Peeking around the corner, I noticed Ruby standing over Nancy's shoulder, facing me. I set my phone on the floor and pressed the record button. Between my ghost and the phone, we should have an accurate record of the discussion.

"Thanks for meeting me today," Nancy said. "I'm very concerned about Belinda."

"Why don't you tell me what's going on?"

"Well, first and foremost, she's drinking a lot. And she's starting to hurt herself."

"Hurting herself?!" O'Malley exclaimed. "What does that mean?"

"Yesterday she took a tumble down the stairs leading to the pool and banged up her knee and hands pretty badly. The other day she bumped into a wall and now has a huge bruise there."

"Because of her drinking?"

"Yes. She needs help."

"Let's clear her of the murder charge first and then concentrate on her other issue, okay?"

"I don't know if that's a good idea," Nancy said. "I think a two-pronged approach may be better. She's talking about buying yachts and airplanes now that Harold's gone. I'm afraid she's so out of her mind with grief, she's acting irresponsibly. I'd hate to see her make rash decisions. I feel like she needs some boundaries and guidance from someone who isn't as affected by Harold's death."

"What did you have in mind?" O'Malley asked.

"I think she needs to be deemed mentally unfit. At least for a little while until she gets the help she needs."

A long silence stretched on and I peeked around the cabinets. O'Malley's back was to me, while Nancy stared at him, her brow furrowed in worry. Ruby was nowhere in sight. She'd probably become bored and decided to head off to her tunnel or go sit with Elvira.

"And what proof do you have that's necessary?" he asked. "It's quite the serious path to take."

"Belinda's had an alcohol problem for a number of months," Nancy said. "Harold's death has only exacerbated it. She's falling down in public, which has been documented by the hotel security staff. The bruise on her arm... Here, look."

I imagined Nancy pulling out a cell phone and showing the damage to O'Malley. I didn't dare peek around the cabinet again.

"Now all this talk about extravagant spending while in the depths of her grief... She's out of her mind. She needs help. Not only through medical means, but also with her finances. She's told me she doesn't have any idea how much money she has or where it is. All these things need to be sorted."

"We can hire a financial planner for that," O'Malley said. "As for the drinking... Well, I'm not sure how to proceed in getting her help if she doesn't want it."

"By declaring her incompetent," Nancy insisted. "She's a ticking timebomb waiting to go off. Either she'll hurt herself both physically and financially, or someone will take advantage of her."

An icy chill ran over my arm and I looked over to find Ruby sitting next to me. "What are you doing?" she asked, grinning.

I brought my finger up to my lips, hoping she'd be quiet so I could concentrate.

"Look, I care about my friend," Nancy continued. "She's... she's like my sister. I don't want to see anything happen to her."

Was she crying?

"I'm... I'm sorry," she said, sniffing. "My friend's hurting and I don't know what to do about it."

"It's okay," O'Malley said. "There's got to be a tissue around here somewhere."

Please see the box of tissue on the side table. Don't come in here looking for some!

"Here you go," he said.

"What can I do to help her?" Nancy asked a moment later.

"I'm not really sure," O'Malley said. "I suppose being there for her during this difficult time is about all there is."

"What if... what if... oh, never mind. I had an idea, but it's dumb."

"No, please. Tell me. As I say to my little girl, there aren't any dumb questions or ideas."

"I was just thinking... What if I became her

guardian or something like that? I could help keep her life afloat, pay her bills until she gets the counseling she needs?"

"Hmm... are you saying you want power of attorney instated?"

"I... I don't know the legal jargon. Power of attorney, co-signer on the accounts... whatever is going to make Belinda's life easier right now. At least until she's back on her feet and in a better state of mind."

"Well, we can't do that without her permission."

"I can talk to her," Nancy said. "If you think it's a good idea."

"And if she doesn't agree?" O'Malley asked. "What then?"

"Perhaps we should think about her seeing a doctor when we get back to Los Angeles," Nancy suggested. "It breaks my heart, but she's at rock bottom. She's overwhelmed and I'm afraid it's all too much for her."

"We'll be able to leave in the next few days. I actually spoke to the sheriff's office and they claimed they're close to making an arrest."

"Oh, really?"

"Yes," O'Malley said. "It's obviously one of those unsavory characters who were in the Jeep."

"I'm sure you're right," Nancy agreed. "I

wouldn't put it past that driver, Jack, either. He knew the area well, and it was nighttime. Even with the moon, one would have to be aware of the terrain. At least be very athletic."

"I'm not worried about which one they arrest, as long as it's not you or Belinda."

"Thank you," Nancy said, sniffing again. "I'm so thankful you're here. This trip has been such a nightmare, and I'm so concerned about Belinda... I don't know what to do."

"You're a good friend to her, Nancy," O'Malley said. "Everyone should be so lucky."

"Thank you for your time."

I peeked around the cabinet to find her and O'Malley standing. He motioned her to the front door. It was time to sneak back into my bedroom and listen to what I'd recorded.

"You better make like a crab and scurry away before he comes in here," Ruby said. "He's going to need a stiff drink after that dramafest."

I grabbed my phone and crawled on my hands and knees into my bedroom, then quietly shut the door. Elvira watched me from the bed as I stood, her hooded stare indicating a lot of judgment.

"Yes, I know I shouldn't have done that," I whispered. "Quit looking at me like I just killed someone."

"So, what did you think?" Ruby asked, wrapping herself around the feline, who shut her eyes and began to purr loudly.

"Nancy is really worried about Belinda," I whispered, sinking into the rocking chair. I didn't want another episode of a guest overhearing my conversation with a ghost.

"Is she?"

I furrowed my brow. "What do you mean?"

"Is she worried, or is she a snake in the grass?"

"How in the world did you come up with that idea? She seemed very concerned about her friend's drinking and her future. She wants to make sure Belinda doesn't do anything stupid in her state of grief."

"I don't know about that, Bernie. What if she's trying to get her hands on Belinda's money? I mean, having your friend declared incompetent based on the fact she's drunk because her husband died? What kind of nonsense is that?"

Pursing my lips together, I reflected on Ruby's theory. I had considered Nancy having ulterior motives as well but her sincerity seemed so real, I couldn't imagine her having anything but goodness in her heart. But then again, I wasn't nearly as jaded as Ruby.

"And I don't even know if she's drunk," Ruby continued. "From what I saw, I can understand her being a little tipsy off of two glasses of wine, but not stumbling around and running into walls so bad, her arm looks like she was hit with a baseball bat."

"What do you think is going on?" I asked, now intrigued.

"I have no idea, but I think we better go back to the hotel and snoop around a little more."

My stomach flipped just thinking about hiding out in the hotel hallway again. Security had come so close to catching me before.

When the phone vibrated in my hand, it startled me so badly, I almost threw it across the room as if it were a snake.

"You need to unknot those knickers of yours," Ruby said. "Who is it?"

A number I didn't recognize scrolled across the screen. I almost didn't answer, but then I saw it originated in Idaho. "Hello?"

"Is this Bernadette?"

"Yes, but you can call me Bernie. Can I ask who's speaking?"

"Bernie, my name's Vicky Darling. I'm Darla's mom."

"I'm so glad you called," I said, absolutely relieved to have something else to think about besides a murder. "How is she?"

"It takes time for the medications to work, but she seems a little more in touch."

"That's fantastic. Is there anything I can do to help her?"

"Not right now," Vicky said, sighing. "I also spoke to the guy who called me... Jack. He's told me everything Darla has done. It didn't surprise me, but at the same time, she used to tell me about you and how much she liked being your friend. When she's out of the hospital and feeling better, I hope you'll have compassion for her."

Darla had hurt me, but I could easily forgive her, especially since I now understood the root of the issue. "Of course. I can't wait to see her."

"It's going to be a while before I can allow that to happen," Vicky explained. "I wish she'd never moved away from home. She actually chose to live in Sedona because she believed the vortexes would help her condition. I hated having her in another state, but she seemed to be doing so well the past few years."

"Until now."

"Yes, until now. I had a feeling she was off her meds. The paranoid talk of you trying to take her boyfriend who appeared out of nowhere worried me, but she assured me she was fine."

"She never told me about the medication or the schizophrenia," I said. "I never understood where her accusations came from. They seemed ridiculous to me, and then she just became nasty."

"I'm so sorry about that, Bernie. Between you and Jack, she's got some great friends here. I hope you'll both be able to forgive her."

"That won't be a problem for me."

"I'll keep you posted on how she's doing," Vicky said. "Again, thank you for being such a wonderful friend to my daughter."

I hung up the phone and stared at it a moment, missing Darla. I'd loved our chats and hanging out together. Maybe she'd be able to whip me back into shape when she was feeling better. Hanging out with Ruby, I'd become quite lazy and it was starting to show.

"Earth to Bernie," Ruby said. "Let's get back to the task at hand, shall we?"

I sighed and glanced over at my ghost. "And what's that? You seem to think Nancy is some psycho who wants Belinda's money while she strikes me as nothing but a very concerned friend."

"Humor me. Let's go back to the hotel and prove me wrong."

With a groan, I set down my phone and placed my head in my hands. Maybe my initial suspicions about Nancy had been correct—she wasn't a concerned friend but wanted access to Belinda's money. If so, she was one heck of an actress and had me questioning myself. I needed time to think and I needed to talk to Adam about the recording.

But then again, what if Ruby was right? What if Nancy had an elaborate plan to take Belinda's money?

"I'll consider going back to the hotel," I muttered. "After I speak with Adam."

"Okay, fine. What time are you talking to the copper?"

"I don't know. As soon as he can meet me."

"Can we go to his house?"

"Why?"

Ruby shrugged. "I want to see Ned. He's kind of cute... for a dead guy."

Oh, no. Was Ruby becoming sweet on Ned?

CHAPTER SIXTEEN

Adam invited me to an early morning coffee at his house the next day. I left a pot on in my own kitchen and set out a plate of donuts with a note to Mr. O'Malley to help himself. Not exactly the best host, but Adam and I had a murder to solve.

Ruby whisked through his door before me, oddly quiet. I knocked and he opened the panel right away.

"It's good to see you," he said, embracing me.

"You as well."

"Coffee?"

"Oh, yes," I said. "It's desperately needed."

"So what happened yesterday?" he asked, leading me to the couch. We hadn't been able to talk the previous evening because Adam had worked late once again. He wasn't confident our conversation would remain private at the station. *The walls have ears*, he'd said.

"I recorded the discussion between Nancy and the lawyer," I replied.

Adam arched a brow. "You shouldn't have told me. That's illegal."

"Don't remind me," I grumbled. "But before you listen to it, I wanted to see Belinda's statement."

"Sure." Adam rose from the couch and hurried into the kitchen, returning a few moments later with two steaming mugs and his laptop. "If we're breaking laws, it's best to make sure we shatter them all."

I took a long sip of the brew and sighed. Nectar of the gods, especially in the early morning hours.

"Here you go," Adam said, handing me the device. "This is the second interview we did with Belinda. I couldn't believe it, but she showed up drunk."

"Really?"

"Yes. She was slurring her words and seemed like she was about to pass out."

"It's bold showing up for an interview in that condition."

"Or stupid."

I always believed a fine line existed between stupid and bold, and sometimes they were one and the same. "Maybe both?" After another gulp, I set the cup down and focused on the screen. "Thanks for the coffee, Adam. Delicious."

"You're welcome. Keep in mind that during the interview we're showing Belinda a map of the cliff."

Q: Thanks for coming in again, Belinda. Can you go over what happened the night of your husband's death?

A: *Harold and those men argued when I asked them to lower their voices because I couldn't hear the tour operator.*

Q: And what transpired when you got to the top of the cliff?

A: *Harold and I walked toward the moon. It was so big and beautiful. Like a huge face in the sky. Everyone went different ways.*

Q: So you and Harold walked over here. Is that correct?

A: *Yes. A little trail led to the overlook. The moon lit it well. I had to get away from the rest of the group.*

. . .

Q: You and Harold were admiring the moon. Then what happened?

A: *We were close to the edge and I began to feel a little woozy. I returned to the Jeep.*

Q: Did you two argue while you were by the edge?

A: *No. Harold barely spoke to me. When he's upset, he gets quiet.*

Q: I thought he was yelling and insulting everyone?

A: *That was before. After, he was quiet.*

Q: That night you had red dirt on your pants. Do you want to tell me how that happened?

A: *I already did.*

Q: Humor me. Tell me again.

A: *I was heading back to the Jeep and I tripped and fell.*

. . .

Q: Are you sure?

A: *Of course I'm sure.*

Q: There wasn't a scuffle between you and your husband? And you fell during that?

A: *Are you insinuating I killed my husband?*

Q: We have to ask, ma'am.

A: *How dare you! I didn't kill Harold!*

Q: Let's get back on track. You and your husband walked over to the ledge. You admired the moon for a bit, then you began heading back to the Jeep where you fell. Correct?

A: *Yes.*

Q: The driver, Jack, doesn't recall seeing you back at the Jeep.

A: *I was there before he whistled for everyone to return! I was there! I had sat on a rock near the back, a few feet away from the bumper!*

•   •   •

Q: Are you okay, Belinda?

A: *I'm sorry. I don't feel well.*

"WAS SHE UPSET DURING THE INTERVIEW?" I asked.

Adam nodded. "She was either crying or indignant. Reading the transcript doesn't give the proper nuance of the meeting."

I imagined her in floods of tears one moment, screaming the next, most likely caused by the alcohol. "Was O'Malley there with her?"

"Yes. He shut it down when she mentioned she was ill."

"Do you think she murdered Harold?"

"I don't know, Bernie. I mean, she admits she went to the ledge with her husband. She's got the best motive and the most to gain out of anyone who was there. But then again, she's obviously grieving."

"Or she's the best actress around."

"Yes, that could be the case as well."

I stood and walked into the kitchen to refill my cup. When I returned, Adam asked, "Can we go over what happened yesterday at your place?"

"Sure. Do you want to listen to it?"

He sighed and shook his head. "Yeah, but I'm

breaking the law by doing so."

"It's still up for debate whether you're breaking the law by having a ghost spy on the suspects."

"Agreed, but this is *definitely* a rule breaker."

We stared at each other for a long moment and finally, he shrugged. "Just give me the rundown on what happened. I can't bring myself to listen to the recording."

Once finished, I said, "Ruby thinks Nancy is a snake in the grass and wants Belinda's money. To me, she comes across as a concerned friend. I'm not sure who's correct."

I fully expected Ruby to make an appearance and declare herself the winner, but she didn't. Where in the world had she gone?

"It's impossible for Nancy to have killed Harold," Adam said. "They were on the upper left of the cliff, Nancy was on the lower left. She'd have to walk right by Jack to find the trail leading to Harold."

"And he didn't mention that?"

Adam shook his head. "I mean, it's *possible* she made it past Jack without being seen, but not very likely."

"Belinda said she came back to the Jeep and sat on a rock near the bumper," I said. "She'd see Nancy as well."

"And she never mentioned it."

"What if they're in on it together?" I asked. "Just thinking aloud."

"Nancy doesn't have a motive to kill Harold."

"Except a long and deep friendship with a woman who was married to a jerk."

Adam sighed and ran his hand through his hair. "Maybe Belinda promised her a big payout for killing Harold?"

"It's possible. Or maybe they're in love and wanted Harold out of the way. I always found it odd that a married couple would stay in the same hotel room as a single woman. I could understand if finances were an issue, but in this case, they aren't. Perhaps Belinda insisted on having Nancy stay with them."

Adam sprung to his feet and began to pace. "I never considered that angle."

As Adam walked off his frustration, I had nothing to add. I wished I could wave a magic wand and solve this case for him just so he'd have a little peace in his heart. Being in charge of finding the killer was eating at him, especially since the investigation was at a complete standstill and he was relying on a not-very-reliable ghost and her granddaughter to solve the case.

When Ruby had suggested going back to the hotel to spy on Nancy and Belinda, my original reaction had been to shut it down because I'd almost been caught by security. However, I recognized Belinda and Nancy were the keys to breaking this case wide open. Adam needed me to take Ruby back there. How he proved whatever evidence we discovered would be up to him.

But I didn't want to be arrested for trespassing. My record was squeaky clean, and I had every intention of keeping it that way. I'd already lied by omission to O'Malley by not sharing that I was actually a witness in the investigation involving his two clients, and I'd recorded a privileged conversation. Bile rose in my throat as I considered how many laws I'd broken to help Adam. Was I willing to go even further?

And what if I was arrested at the hotel? Would it matter? I supposedly had law enforcement on my side, but if it came right down to it, how far would Adam go to protect me?

I wasn't sure I liked the waters where our relationship had ventured. Seemingly, I was the one taking the risks while in the end, he'd get the rewards.

But I wanted to help Adam.

Jeez, I hated this.

"Ruby wants to go back to the hotel and spy on Nancy and Belinda some more," I said. "I'm not sure it's a good idea though. I'm on security's radar. If I'm caught outside Belinda's door, it could ruin the case, especially if O'Malley is able to put you and me together. A conversation with the right people in town would verify that we know each other. Heck, if he actually studied the file and looked at the names of those involved, he'd realize he's staying at a witness's house."

"Not a very hotshot lawyer, is he? And us knowing each other doesn't make us guilty of anything."

"Some would say we're dating," I said, shrugging.

"That's true."

But now I was uncertain. Weren't we seeing each other? Or had I been horribly mistaken this past month? No, he'd specifically asked me out on a *date*. Perhaps I was overthinking our relationship? Me overthinking something? It wouldn't be the first time.

"What if I went back to the hotel with you?" Adam asked. "I wouldn't be in uniform, but I'd be close by. That way, if you do get caught snooping, I can smooth things over with security."

"How would you know?"

"We'd keep in contact via phone."

Ruby appeared. "Let's go," she said, heading for the front door.

"Where?"

"To the hotel, Sherlock. Let's crack this case for the copper. We know there's stink in the state of Demark, so let's find out who's passing the gas."

Adam glanced around. "Ruby's here?"

"Yes. She wants to go to the hotel right now."

After glancing at the clock on the wall, he stared at me. "I can be late. I just need to call it in. I'll go with you."

The clock read close to eight. There would be a lot of hustle and bustle in the hotel of early morning golfers and hikers, which would make it easier for me to blend in while Ruby snooped. Either that, or people would wonder what the heck I was doing standing outside someone's hotel room. There were only so many times I could bend down to tie my shoe, right?

And what about Belinda? If she was as big of a drinker as everyone claimed, I bet she found it hard to raise her head from the pillow before noon.

But, there was only one way to find out. "Okay, let's go."

CHAPTER SEVENTEEN

When we arrived at the Sedona Grand Hotel, Adam stayed in the lobby while Ruby and I decided to walk the stairs instead of taking the elevator to the second floor. Well, I actually made the choice while Ruby complained about it. How that woman had stayed alive for so long with her hatred of exercise and all her bad habits, I'd never understand.

When we arrived at Belinda and Nancy's room, I assumed my previous position and Ruby ghosted through the door, humming softly to herself. The hallway remained clear for a few long moments, and I began to relax until my phone buzzed in my pocket. I pulled it out and saw Adam was calling. I glanced to my right and to my left but didn't want to take the chance of Belinda and Nancy hearing me speak to him, so I sent it to voicemail.

A few moments later, Ruby exited and motioned me to follow her down the hall.

"What's going on in there?" I asked, my heart thundering.

"Not a lot. Belinda's still in bed moaning about something while Nancy's getting dressed. Her bra and panty set are a little too frilly for me, though. You know, I always preferred to go au naturel. Much more comfortable."

Should I remind her we were in the middle of a murder investigation, not a lingerie show?

"Did Nancy happen to mention where she was going?" I asked.

"Nope. She's getting pretty jazzed up for a trip down for coffee though."

I couldn't imagine where'd she be going besides downstairs. Perhaps she was one of those people who didn't venture out in the morning unless she had on a full face of makeup and was dressed to impress. Unless she'd met someone she wanted to dazzle while she'd been here? And what kind of person found a boyfriend while in the middle of a murder investigation? "We need to find out where she's headed off to," I whispered. "Go back in there and see if she gives any indication to Belinda so then we can sneak ahead of her."

"Aye-aye, Captain," Ruby said with a salute.

My phone rang again as I followed her back to the room. She moved through the door just as I whispered, "Hello?"

"Retreat! Retreat!" Ruby yelled, returning to the hallway. "Run for your life!"

My phone call forgotten, I shoved it into my pocket and sprinted down the hallway, then rounded the corner as I heard a door closed. I peeked around to find Nancy heading my way.

Panic gripped me as I looked for a place to hide. The elevator was to my left and Nancy was coming my way to my right. There was nowhere for me to go. I was trapped and Nancy would find me in seconds.

"The staircase! The staircase!" Ruby screamed. For once, her hysteria was actually useful.

I ran for the door and pushed it open into the cement staircase, then quietly closed it as I stared out the long, rectangular window. Seconds later, Nancy rounded the corner wearing a floral dress and a pair of strappy heels. Definitely dressed to impress... but impress who?

"What if she comes in here?" Ruby whispered.

"What if she's a health nut like you and always takes the stairs?"

In those heels? I doubted it, but Ruby had a valid point. With the assumption that Nancy was heading downstairs for coffee or breakfast, I ran up to the landing of the third floor and peered over the railing, ready to sprint to the top of the dang building if Nancy entered the stairwell.

Long moments passed and the door on the second floor remained closed. "Let's go down to the lobby," I said. "She must be headed there."

"No. Let's go check the elevator first and see what floor lights up. That wasn't breakfast and coffee underwear. Trust me."

I followed my ghost down to the second floor and out into the hallway. The elevator was traveling upward and stopped on the fourth floor. "We don't know if that's her for sure," I said.

"We can make an educated guess, though, Bernie. She got on the elevator, and now it's on the fourth floor. She's visiting someone else."

"What if she went down to the lobby and someone new is on the elevator?"

"Come on," Ruby urged. "Humor a dead woman and let's go up. Run your butt off on the stairs. Isn't that what you always want to do anyway?"

I pushed open the door and sprinted up the stairs to the fourth floor. When I arrived completely winded, I made a promise to myself that I'd get back into shape. No more reruns of *Magnum P.I.* for me. Instead, I'd use the time to exercise.

"Give me a minute," I gasped as I placed my hands on my knees and sucked in the stale stairway air in large gulps.

"Hurry up!" Ruby glanced out the window. "She's probably walking down the hallway!"

I pulled open the door and stepped out to an exact replica of the second floor, except the carpet was rustic red instead of beige. In fact, it reminded me of the color of the Sedona dirt. As I rounded the corner, Nancy was indeed walking down the hall. She stopped in front of a room on the right and knocked, then ran a hand over her dress and fluffed her hair with her fingers.

A second later, a bright smile came over her face and she disappeared into the room. Leaning against the wall I took a deep breath and glanced at Ruby. "What do we do now?"

"She won't be leaving for a while," Ruby said. "Whoever is in that room is going to keep her busy."

"How do you know?"

"That was sexy-time underwear, trust me."

I didn't want to think about Nancy or what exactly that meant. "What now?"

"I'm not setting foot in that room," Ruby said, pointing to where Nancy had gone. "There are certain things even I don't want to see. Let's go back and check on Belinda, but we can take the elevator this time."

As we waited for the doors to part, I listened for approaching footsteps. Unlike Ruby, I wasn't certain about how Nancy was spending her time and I had to believe she'd recognize me if we ran into each other. We'd spent hours sitting across from each other in the sheriff's hallway right after the murder.

When the doors finally opened, we stepped inside and rode down to the second floor.

"Something's not right about Belinda," Ruby said. "She was moaning and groaning, but I don't think she's awake."

"Maybe she was dreaming."

"That's either one heck of a good dream or a nightmare," Ruby replied. "I'll feel better once I get another look around."

I pressed my back against the wall as Ruby once again went into Belinda's room. For a second, I considered calling Adam, but decided against it. I had no idea what Belinda was doing inside. She could be up and about and I didn't want her to hear me, open her door and discover me standing right outside. I had faith she would also recognize me. Instead, I sent him a quick text.

Nancy's up on the 4th floor visiting someone. Belinda's still in bed. Ruby's in Belinda's room. We had a close call but we're safe.

A moment later, my phone buzzed in my pocket. Adam had texted back.

What's she doing on the 4th? Who's she visiting?

Don't know, I typed.

Ruby came through the door and stood directly in front of me. "Belinda's still moaning in the bed. I took a good look around and found some pills in the bathroom. What's flozitepman?"

"I have no idea."

"Maybe it's a cold medicine I've never heard of," Ruby said.

"I'll look it up. Do you remember how to spell it?"

"Heck no. I'm not even sure I said that right. Let me go back in and I'll call out the letters to you."

As Ruby yelled the letters, I typed them in with shaky fingers. Nothing was coming up. Either I was mistyping or she was misreading.

"Did you get it?" she asked, coming back to my side of the door again.

I shook my head and ground my jaw as I tried to hide my irritation. I wasn't sure if the debacle was Ruby's fault or mine, but the whole scenario had my frustration level matching my anxiety. On one hand, I wanted to scream. On the other, I wanted to curl up in a ball and cry, or run from the building. Glancing over my shoulder, I studied the empty hallway, unable to shake the feeling that I was going to get caught. "Go back in there and spell it again. This time be louder, though."

"Watch your tone, Bernie," Ruby chided. "And for both our sakes, try to relax. You're going to worry yourself to death right here on this horrid carpet." I looked down at the light brown flooring. "See what I mean? It reminds me of the color of a filled diaper. You don't want to die here."

After ghosting through the door once again, Ruby called out the spelling, slower this time. I focused on the phone and whispered each letter as I typed it.

When I'd finished, it wasn't *flozitepman* as Ruby had originally said, but *flunitrazepam*. And as I read the description, my blood turned cold and goosebumps crawled over my skin.

"What is it?" Ruby asked. "Is it horrible? The fact that you're so pale makes me think it's really bad."

"It's prescribed for severe insomnia. But it's also a date-rape drug."

"Date-rape drug!" Ruby exclaimed. "What the heck?"

We stared at each other for a moment. Why would Belinda and Nancy have a date-rape drug in their room?

"I'm so confused," I whispered.

Ruby's eyes widened as she glanced over my shoulder. "Let's think about that later," she said. "I think now is a good time to run."

As I turned around, I found Art and Nancy striding toward me, both of their gazes fixed on me. There was no time to contemplate what the heck the two of them were doing together, and hiding wasn't an option. My flight response, which had been humming along at just above neutral, shifted into high gear. A string of curses fell from my lips and I sprinted down the hall away from them, figuring at some point I'd find another staircase.

Heavy footsteps sounded behind me, as well as Ruby's screams. "Faster, Bernie! Make like the wind!"

I peeked back to find Art gaining on me. Dang, the man was fast. I had a pretty good head start and he had covered the space in record time.

Rounding the corner, I searched for the stairwell and hoped I could reach it and maybe lock myself in. My chest heaved and burned as I forced myself to run faster.

A thump sounded behind me and I looked over my shoulder. Art had come around the corner and hit the wall, which slowed him down a little bit.

I sprinted as fast as I could and noted the elevators up on my right, which I hoped meant a staircase. If not, Art would have me trapped at the end of the hallway with nowhere for me to go but out the window that probably didn't open.

When I saw the door, tears sprung to my eyes. I burst through it. Art had gained on me once again and I didn't have time to see if I could lock him out. My only hope was reaching the lobby where people were bustling about. He wouldn't do anything in the presence of a group of witnesses, right?

My footsteps pounded down the concrete stairs almost as loud as my heart. Glancing up, I spotted Art above me. Then he did something right out of an action flick. He threw himself over the railing and landed just a few inches behind me. I screamed when his fingers gripped my shoulders and pulled me down on the concrete landing.

Ruby shrieked and cursed while I struggled to free myself. "Get away from my granddaughter, you ugly son of a cow face!"

Within seconds, Art straddled me and had my arms pinned against the floor. "Why are you running?" he asked as I fought to catch my breath. "Why are you outside Nancy's room?"

"Name, rank, and serial number only!" Ruby screamed, her ghostly hands slapping Art's head from behind.

I wasn't about to explain that my dead grandmother was spying on Belinda and Nancy. "Get off me!" I yelled.

Art cuffed a hand over my mouth so hard, my ears rang for a long moment. "Quiet. What's your name again?"

"Don't say a word!" Ruby yelled. She obviously didn't realize I couldn't even if I wanted to with Art's hand blocking my mouth. I tried to bite him, but he had my jaw clamped so tight, I couldn't move it.

"Fine," he said. "We'll go back to Nancy's room and have a chat. I'm going to let you up. If you so much as breathe too heavily, I'll drag your scrawny butt up to the top of the stairwell and toss you to the bottom. Do you understand me?"

I nodded and a nervous giggle escaped. Scrawny? For some reason, it made me laugh, which was dumb since he'd just threatened my life. But I'd been feeling so chunky lately, the description brought a little levity to the fact that I could very well die.

"Let's go," Art ordered. "And remember what I told you."

CHAPTER EIGHTEEN

"You're lucky I'm not alive, or I'd have you singing soprano," Ruby yelled as we walked back to Nancy's room. "Kick him where it hurts, Bernie! Then run!"

Art gripped my arm so tightly, I bit back the pain. I had no doubt there'd be a bruise. Even if I could wrench away from him and land a swift foot to his nether region, I didn't have the confidence that I could outrun him. He'd proven he could catch me, and being dropped four stories in a stairwell wasn't exactly the way I wanted to go.

"You need some self-defense classes," Ruby said. "Let's put that on the to-do list."

When we arrived at Nancy and Belinda's hotel room, Art knocked quietly. The door flew open seconds later and Nancy glared at me.

"What's her story?" she asked, stepping aside.

"I'm not sure yet, but we aren't leaving any loose ends."

He pushed me toward the table and motioned for me to sit. Two matching queen beds with brown and red comforters sat in the middle of the room, separated by a nightstand. Belinda lay in the bed closest to the window, completely unaware of everything going on around her. As Nancy and Art conferred by the door, I slipped out my phone and quickly hit redial, then shoved it into my back pocket. When I heard Adam's tinny voice, I coughed to cover the sound. Art and Nancy glared at me, then she marched over and placed her palms flat on the table, staring down at me mob movie style.

"What are you doing here?" she asked.

"Art chased me down and threatened to drop me down a four-story stairwell if I didn't allow him to bring me to your room, Nancy," I said, hoping Adam had stayed on the line. "You tell me what I'm doing here."

Nancy glanced over her shoulder. "We should've let her go. We have everything we need."

"I told you, we can't leave any loose ends," Art growled. "We're so close to this being over."

I studied the room. Based on the pile of towels in

the corner and the garbage overflowing in the canister, housekeeping hadn't paid a visit in a while. And why was Belinda asleep with all these people in the room?

There was only one answer I could think of: Nancy had been drugging her.

But why?

"How long have you known Art?" I asked Nancy. "It seems like you've been acquainted for a lot longer than you've been in Sedona."

Nancy turned back to me and smiled. "That's really none of your business, and honestly, the less you know the better."

"I see you're drugging your friend with the date-rape drug you have," I ventured.

Her face paled and she narrowed her gaze. "How do you know?"

"Well, she's out cold and I saw the flunitrazepam on the bathroom sink when I walked in." Not true, but it sounded far more plausible than telling her my ghost had found it. "It was an educated guess."

Where the heck was Adam? Had he hung up and not heard any of this conversation? Would I meet my end by being tossed over the stairwell railing?

"She knows too much," Nancy said.

"I figured," Art snapped. "Like I said, loose ends."

Crud. I had to keep them talking and pray Adam would arrive soon, because I honestly knew very little. If Adam was still listening, the whole case could be unraveled and hopefully I wouldn't die.

So... what did I know with certainty? Nancy knew Art. They had a familiarity about them and as Ruby had pointed out, the woman had gotten prettied up to meet him, as though they had some kind of romantic attachment.

Belinda had been drugged. I considered all the times someone had mentioned Belinda had been drunk and was pretty sure she'd been under the influence of the flunitrazepam, not a glass of wine or two.

But why?

"Everything's in order," Nancy said, grinning at Art. "Do what you have to do and let's get out of here. Los Angeles is screaming for me to come home."

"And Sedona is screaming at you to get the heck out of dodge, buttercup," Ruby said standing nose to nose with the woman. "If I were alive, I'd bloody that condescending smile of yours."

"What's that smell?" Nancy muttered. Ruby brought her fists up and ghost-boxed her face.

"And if you touch my granddaughter, I won't rest until every ghost left on this planet is terrorizing you," Ruby continued. "I'll find a poltergeist who wants to live under your bed and licks your toes while you try to sleep."

As Nancy sat down in the chair across from me, Art chuckled and placed a kiss on her head. "Patience, honey. We don't want to move too fast and draw attention to ourselves."

"Just get me out of this horrid town."

Both stared at me and Art shook his head. "How is this going to work? We can pull the drug overdose on Belinda, but I'm not sure about her."

"Oh! I know!" Nancy exclaimed. "We'll drug her, then put them in bed together! A lovers' suicide! Or drug overdose. It doesn't matter what the cops think as long as we're in Bora Bora by the time they untangle this web we've weaved."

"Why are you killing your best friend?" I asked.

"For her money, of course," Nancy said. "Don't be stupid, dear."

"You killed Harold then?" I asked, remembering the drawing of the cliffs Adam had made. Nancy had been at the lower left side while Harold had been at the upper left. She'd have to make it past Jack and Belinda to get to Harold without being seen.

"No. Have you ever heard the term, brains and brawn?"

I nodded and glanced over at Art. With his build, he definitely met the definition of brawn.

"In this case, I'm the brains," Nancy said, a sweet smile crossing her face.

I wasn't too sure about that. Art seemed to be calling the shots, but I wouldn't argue her perceived role.

Art and Trevor had been on the upper right side of the cliff. Art's athletic ability he'd so gallantly displayed while chasing me down would have allowed him to cross the rocky terrain with ease. He'd fought Harold with the brute strength that had left my body bruised.

"She knows enough," Art said. "Quit talking, Nancy."

"Don't tell me what to do!" Nancy stood and glared at him, her hands on her hips. "I'm the one in charge here! I'm the one who has worked for years to make this plan come together!"

The plan? I fully appreciated she wanted Belinda's money, but I didn't understand how this whole strategy was organized. How did she plan on making a grab for Belinda's bank accounts when the woman on the bed couldn't keep her eyes open?

"Hey, Bernie!" Ruby said. I glanced over to find her standing beside the bed, right next to Belinda. Her worry over my safety had been overshadowed by whatever had caught her attention. "Over here on the nightstand is a bunch of papers Belinda signed. It looks like she's made Nasty Nancy a co-signer on all her bank accounts."

And there it was. She'd drugged Belinda and hoped to have her deemed unfit, but when O'Malley hadn't jumped on board with that idea, she'd forced Belinda to sign, then kept her so out of it, she couldn't stay awake long enough to fight it, legally or otherwise.

And now, Nancy was going to kill her with a drug overdose. No one would catch on until Nancy was busy spending the money in Bora Bora. I personally would have chosen France or Italy, but to each their own.

"Just get this over with!" Nancy yelled as she marched toward the bathroom, Ruby right behind her muttering something about the woman's face resembling a dog's behind. Art wouldn't meet my gaze.

"She's crushing a pill!" Ruby shouted. "No! She's

crushing four! Holy cow! Bernie, don't drink this water she's bringing out!"

"I thought you may be thirsty," Nancy said sweetly when she emerged from the bathroom and set the glass in front of me.

"Actually, I'm fine," I said, pushing the glass across the table toward her.

"You look parched," she said, sliding it back toward me.

As Ruby screamed at me, I picked up the glass and threw the water in Nancy's face. She gasped while I raced for the door. Art quickly wrapped his arm around my waist and flung me back into the chair, sending my head against the wall with a loud thump. As stars appeared before my eyes, my phone slipped out of my back pocket and landed on the carpet with a thud.

I wasn't sure how much time had passed, but finally, I was able to focus on Nancy, who stood over me with another glass, her mascara in long streaks down her face. I smiled, her ruined makeup job bringing me a little bit of joy on an otherwise horrible day.

"Don't drink it," Ruby said, standing right next to Nancy. "She drugged it again."

"Hold her in place," Nancy ordered.

Art came around the side of the table and tossed it toward the door. Grabbing my ponytail, he yanked my head back while Nancy gripped my jaw and poured the water in my mouth. I struggled against Art, kicked at Nancy and tried to breathe and spit up as much of the water as possible. The horrid sensation of drowning and not being able to get enough air burned my lungs while Ruby's screams of terror and empty threats of violence filled my ears. She couldn't help me.

If I died, would I be trapped in this hotel room, like Ruby had been trapped in our house? Would she be confined with me?

Oh, my word... Ruby and I trapped in this hotel room for all eternity? No. Absolutely not. I loved my grandmother, but everyone had their limits.

My renewed urge to escape dimmed as my head became horribly foggy, as though a storm had suddenly moved into my brain. I'd had to swallow some of the water and it had gone directly to my head. Blackness encroached on my peripheral vision. My arms and legs became heavy and difficult to move.

The scene seemed to fade away, yet I kept on attempting to spit up as much of the water as I could. Nancy let go of my jaw as my eyes closed and my head fell to the left. I didn't have the strength to hold it upright any longer.

"Put her on the bed," Nancy ordered, her voice seemingly on another plane. I was lifted, unable to move, and then bounced when my body hit the mattress. Ruby's cries and threats faded as darkness overtook me.

The last thing I remember before completely passing out was Ruby crying, "Don't you die on me, Bernie!"

CHAPTER NINETEEN

Beep. Beep. Beep.

I flung my arm over to my side table, searching for the stupid alarm clock. The incessant noise refused to stop and finally, I pried open my eyes. Surprisingly, there wasn't an alarm clock to be found, and I wasn't tucked into my own bed.

I was in... a hospital?

Barely able to stay awake, I glanced around the room and found Ruby perched on the end of my bed. A large grin spread over her face as our gazes met.

"Well, hello," she said softly. "You gave this dead lady quite the scare."

I struggled to remember how I'd come to be in a hospital hooked up to an IV, but the memories seemed just out of reach. "Why am I here?" I whispered, my voice hoarse.

"Because that dog face, Nasty Nancy, drugged you. They had to pump your stomach, which was pretty gross and something I wish I didn't have to see. It was touch and go for a while. That horse face tried to kill you, Bernie."

As I stared at the ceiling, everything slowly came back to me. I recalled being tossed on the bed, and then blackness. "Who found me?" Ruby had been helpless to do anything during that situation.

"Adam. I didn't realize you'd called him, but he heard everything. Very sneaky, Bernie. Very sneaky. Saved your hide with that move."

The phone. I remembered dialing and the phone falling out of my pocket when Art slammed me down into the chair. "What took him so long?"

"I'm not sure, but when he arrived with the two beefy security guards we'd run into the previous day, it was like the cavalry or a band of superheroes crashed through the door."

"Thank goodness," I whispered and closed my eyes.

A cold feeling settled over my hand, and I knew Ruby had laid hers on top of mine. Despite the chill, I found it comforting, and drifted off to sleep.

The next time I woke, Adam was sitting on my bed in his tan sheriff's uniform, staring at me with a furrowed brow. "Hey," he said softly. "I'm so glad to see you. Are you okay?"

Since I could barely keep my eyes open and I had an IV, I assumed that perhaps I was okay? I also didn't have the energy to answer, so I shrugged in response.

"I'm so sorry, Bernie," he said, taking my palm in his. "I can't... I can't begin to tell you how awful I feel. I never should have agreed to allow you to help me."

"Don't be silly," I said. "I wanted to."

He shook his head and looked away. I noted his jaw grinding. Was it anger? Distress? Whatever it was, I hated seeing him that way.

"Hey," I said. "We caught the bad guys, right?"

"Darn tootin' we did," Ruby said. I hadn't noticed her standing on the other side of my bed by my head. And she shouldn't have startled me considering she was tied to me, but she had.

"We did," Adam said. "It was smart calling me and leaving the phone on. I have to admit, I almost hung up because I thought you'd accidently dialed, but something told me not to."

"I'm glad you didn't." A chill ran down my spine

when I considered that I could be dead instead of staring into his pretty green eyes. I squeezed his fingers.

"My guilt runs pretty deep on this one, Bernie," he said. "I'm not going to lie. I was so scared."

"Guilt is a wasted emotion," Ruby said. "Not worth the energy."

I disagreed, but in this case, the guilt was unwarranted. "Please don't feel bad, Adam. I was on board and wanted to help you. It's not like you did anything. *They* did."

"You were there because of me."

"I was there because I wanted to be. Now, tell me what happened."

When Adam received the phone call and realized what he was listening to, he ran across the lobby for the elevators. Security stopped him and demanded to see some ID while questioning why he was on the property. As he explained himself, he also set the phone to speaker and the three of them listened while Nancy and Art confessed, then tossed me around. They joined him in the race to the hotel room. Security opened the door for Adam and stopped Art from trying to escape while Adam called an ambulance and subdued the hysterical Nancy. "She kept screaming about how she'd worked so hard for the money, how much she'd endured, and how she didn't deserve to go to jail," Adam said. "Then she had the nerve to blame Art and Trevor for everything."

"Trevor?"

"Yes. Trevor was in on it, mainly along for the ride. He and Art met in prison in Seattle."

Prison! The new knowledge shouldn't have surprised me, but it did. "What were they in for?"

"One for armed robbery, the other for extortion."

"Why didn't any of that come up during their background checks after the murder?" Ruby asked. "Or did the police botch that one up and not do a background check?"

Great question, which I repeated.

"No, we ran them. Art and Trevor gave us fake last names and social security numbers. They had thought ahead and came prepared."

Interesting. But it still didn't explain how Nancy had become acquainted with Art. She didn't seem to be one who associated with men in jail, especially ones located two states away. I didn't understand how they'd all ended up finding each other.

"How did she meet Art?"

"Her stepbrother, a guy named Phillip, was in the same prison and became friendly with Art.

Nancy sent some family photos, and Art happened to notice them. He thought she was pretty and they started corresponding. Art and Trevor were both released within the last year. The rest is history."

I couldn't help but wonder if Nancy had recruited Art for her scheme, or if she had really liked him.

"How long had they been planning the murder?"

"Well, from what I gather, at least three months. When Belinda invited Nancy to travel with them, Nancy saw the opportunity. She had to stay close to Belinda and Harold, so she asked to bunk with them, claiming she was scared of sleeping by herself in a strange hotel. They agreed to the arrangement, and she was able to keep Belinda mildly drugged during their stay until after Harold died. That way, she had proof that Belinda had been acting strange for a while, not just after the death of her husband.

"What's interesting is Nancy, Art, and Trevor weren't sure exactly when Harold would be killed. The Jeep tour turned out to be the perfect time to murder him, so Nancy had Art and Trevor book the tour at the same time as them. They wanted it to look like an accident, and it would have been considered one if we hadn't witnessed the whole thing."

"Talk about being in the right place at the right

time," Ruby muttered, shaking her head.

"Guess Art pushed Harold then, right?"

"Yes. He ran across that terrain we thought would be too difficult to navigate and shoved him over the edge."

Huh. Interesting. Art had threatened to send me over a railing and down four flights of stairs. Not too different from tossing someone off a cliff. "And what did Trevor get out of all this?"

Adam smirked and shook his head. "His job was to travel with Art, to make them look like two guys on a golfing trip. He'd receive a small cut once Nancy had cleaned out Belinda's accounts. Now he's been the most helpful of the group because he doesn't want to go back to prison."

"Belinda!" Oh my gosh. In my haze, I'd almost forgotten about her. "Is she okay?"

"She's got a long road ahead of her," Adam said. "Nancy had been drugging her for at least a week that we know of. She's detoxing, but at least she's alive."

"And she's got all her money," Ruby said. "So she can afford to detox in comfort and luxury."

With a groan, I attempted to sit up and immediately became dizzy and nauseous.

"Put some pillows behind her head, copper!"

Ruby yelled, causing my head to pound.

"Let me help you," Adam murmured. He leaned over and arranged the pillows behind me so I was propped up a bit.

"Thank you," I said.

"Do you want some water?" he asked.

I nodded and glanced around at my sterile white room. The blank television screen stared down at me from the ceiling, the window had the curtains drawn. The smell of disinfectant hung in the air and the low hum of doctors and nurses talking in the hallway was almost as irritating as the beeping machine next to my bed. As a general rule, I hated hospitals and the urge to leave was strong. How was anyone supposed to rest in this environment?

Ruby sat down on my bed and laid her hand over mine again. "I know you aren't feeling well, and I want you to get better. But I was just wondering if you could do it fast because this place gives me the creeps and I want to go home."

"I wholeheartedly agree," I said, also wondering what this stay would do to my bank account. "I want to go home, too."

"Do you know that while I was alive, I went to the doctor a total of twice in my adult life?"

I shook my head, surprised by the revelation.

Who in the world received medical care only twice in her life? "You're kidding me. For what? If you only went two times, it must have been for something pretty serious."

"Oh, yes. First was when I had your mom," she said, holding up her pointer finger. "I walked into the hospital in labor. The next time was after I broke my arm while trying to skateboard when I was fifty." The second finger went up. "Otherwise, I made it through pretty healthy."

"Except for the heart attack that killed you," I reminded her.

"Yeah... except for that."

I wondered if she'd have actually gone to the doctor if the heart attack could have been avoided. With her lifestyle and unwillingness to change, I doubted it.

"I hate doctors," Ruby muttered. "I always believed laughter was the best medicine. It's a fantastic cure. Speaking of which... when you get out of here, let's go to Tip 'Em Back and see Jezebel. She's always good for a hoot."

Tip 'Em Back was the local dive bar Ruby had liked while alive. Owned by Ruby's friend Janis, who died a few years before Ruby, it had been passed down to her granddaughter, a woman named Jezebel.

I'd never visited the place until Ruby suggested we join a poker game there. The night hadn't gone well, and Jezebel had almost kicked me out for cheating. But in the end, we'd bonded over the love for our crazy grandmothers. I wouldn't mind seeing her again. The woman taught self-defense classes on the side, and I made a mental note to contact her.

Adam brought over a small paper cup, then sat down across from Ruby. I sipped greedily, my gaze darting from one to the other. The two people I cared for the most—and one who also drove me absolutely batty—were at my side. Belinda had no one. Her husband had been killed and her so-called best friend had betrayed and hurt her. I couldn't imagine the ache in her heart. Maybe I could go visit her at some point. I wasn't sure what I'd say, but perhaps she'd appreciate the company from someone who had no ill-will toward her.

"Ask the copper how old Nutjob Ned's doing," Ruby said.

I stared at my ghost for a moment, surprised once again she cared. But then I recalled she'd been very diplomatic with Ned and interested in finding out why they were both on this plane. I relayed her question to Adam.

"He's been really quiet," Adam replied, his gaze

set firmly in Ruby's direction. "I haven't been home much, but I haven't sensed any trace of him while I've been there."

Ruby's gaze narrowed. "Did the copper chase off the nutjob?"

"He said he hasn't been home, Ruby," I said. "He hasn't had time to chase off Ned. There was a murder that needed to be solved."

I still found it endearing that Adam talked in the general direction of Ruby, even though he couldn't see or hear her. Acknowledging that she existed meant a lot to my grandmother, and frankly, it did to me, too. Adam and I shared our knowledge of her existence, and he didn't think I was crazy.

"You better get some sleep," he said. "The more you rest, the sooner you'll be able to leave."

"If that's the case, close those eyes," Ruby encouraged. "I'll stand guard. Get better, Bernie, so we can go home."

Adam kissed my forehead and waved as he walked out the door. With a sigh, I shut my eyes. Even with my noisy environment, I did hope to sleep with my crazy, dead grandmother standing over me.

I felt like the luckiest girl in the world.

Two months had gone by, and I'd seen Darla three times. She wasn't quite back to her old self, but she had reopened Darling's Diner and no longer thought I was out to sabotage her life in any way. We'd had a couple of good talks where I'd made it clear that I was her friend and only wanted what was best for her. She'd apologized for her behavior, although it hadn't been necessary. Slowly and surely, we were rebuilding our friendship while Darla worked on getting better.

Per Ruby's request, I had started self-defense classes with Jezebel, the owner of Tip 'Em Back. In her forties, she'd wanted to be a professional MMA fighter, but was never quite good enough. She wore her blonde hair in a ponytail, her body chiseled and her stare intimidating. With her gruff voice, full sleeve tattoo on her left arm, and lack of a smile, she'd actually scared me during our first session, but I reminded myself she wasn't going to beat me up: she was there to teach me how to do that to others. After a few weeks, I considered her a new friend and we often went together to get smoothies after our workouts. I certainly felt stronger, but I wasn't sure I had the confidence to actually use the moves I was learning if the situation were to arise. I hoped I'd never have to find out.

I had been in the process of cleaning guest rooms when a knock sounded at my door. For a moment, I panicked, thinking I'd forgotten a reservation. I checked my phone for a notification of someone checking in, but there wasn't one. For a brief second, relief flooded through me, quickly followed by dread. I hated walk-ins.

To my surprise, Darla was standing on my doorstep, tears rolling down her face, her whole body trembling.

"Darla, what's wrong?" I said, taking her hand and pulling her inside to the couches. Once we sat down, she couldn't meet my gaze, but she continued to cry as she tucked her blonde hair behind her ears.

"Take some deep breaths," I coaxed, gently laying my hand on her shoulder.

She stared off into space and breathed in and out, long and slow. After a moment, she turned to me. "I'm in trouble."

"Tell me what's the matter." I gave her what I hoped was a reassuring half-smile.

"I need your help, Bernie. Please tell me you'll help me."

Dread filled me at her tone. "You know I will, Darla. Please! What's wrong?! I'll do anything for you."

"I went to open the diner this morning."

Staring at her expectantly, I waited for her to state the horrible, awful thing she wanted me to help her with. A spider? The cooler had gone down? A plugged-up dishwasher? She ran out of ketchup?

"And the police were there," she said.

"What did they want?"

"To question me about a murder."

My stomach dropped.

"I didn't do it, Bernie! I swear to you, I didn't!"

"Do the police think you did?"

"They said I was a suspect," she continued, tears streaming down her face.

Oh, no.

Dear Reader,

Please check out Ruby and Bernie's next adventure in The Fiancé is Finished.

When a man is found dead in a hotel room and Darla becomes one of the main suspects, Bernie takes it upon herself to find the true killer in order to save her friend.

The Tri-Town Murders

Complete Series

Follow newspaper reporter Tilly and her group of fun, quirky friends as they solve murders in a fictional, small town in California.

News and Nectarines

News and Nachos

News and Nutmeg

News and Noodles

Killer Skies Mysteries

Set in 1965, join Patty Briggs, stewardess extraordinaire, as she flies the skies and solves murders with the help of her friends... and one cute FBI agent!

ABOUT THE AUTHOR

Carly Winter is the pen name for a USA Today best-selling and award-winning romance author.

When not writing, she enjoys spending time with her family, reading and enjoying the fantastic Arizona weather (except summer - she doesn't like summer). She does like dogs, wine and chocolate and wishes Christmas happened twice a year.

For more information on her books, please visit:
CarlyWinterCozyMysteries.com